My Stand-In Lover

Yuwanda Black

Published by Inkwell Editorial Publishing, 2020.

Copyright © 2020 Yuwanda Black.

All rights reserved.

This is a work of fiction. Similarities to real people, places, or events are entirely coincidental.

MY STAND-IN LOVER

First edition. January 24, 2020.

Written by Yuwanda Black.

PREVIEW

Ditched by a fiance.
Betrayed by a friend.
A desire for revenge.
One life-changing weekend.
***

He'd broken her heart once. Would she give him a chance to break it again?

"What do you want Aaron?" Farrah asked.

"Why are you really here?"

"What if I said I made a mistake letting you go?"

"Wh—what do you mean?" Farrah stammered, not believing her ears. He did not just say that? Did he? Her heart rate picked up speed.

"What if I said I realize what a big mistake it was to let you go?" her ex-fiance, who was scheduled to be married in two days, said.

Aaron walked over to the bed and sat beside Farrah. He took one of her hands in his.

"This doesn't make any sense," Farrah said, almost to herself. His declaration totally threw her off balance. It was the last thing she expected. The very last. She looked at her hand in his. His touch. She'd dreamed about this for months.

And her dream was miraculously coming true, but ...

Was her stand-in lover determined to become a more permanent fixture?
***

The Irishman

Their mating had been vicious, savage, barbaric ... and beautiful. And Farrah wanted more of him. So much more. She hadn't been consumed by this kind of desire since – since forever.

Even Aaron, the man she'd loved for almost a decade, had never come close to making her do some of the things she'd done last night with this perfect stranger.

He was wickedly beautiful.

Sinfully sexy.

Rakishly seductive.

Soulfully encompassing.

And all of this made him the perfect stand-in lover; the perfect man to show up with to her ex-fiance's wedding.

Aaron would be able to smell another man's scent on her. She knew he would because the kind of mind-blowing coupling she'd experienced last night didn't stay confined to the bedroom. It seeped out of your pores and brought a stupid grin to your face for the world to see, smell, crave, and wonder about.

***

Her living room wall served as a bed. He pushed her up against it, lifted her off her feet and slammed himself home one last time – all without breaking the kiss that had ignited it all.

Farrah release was so hard that her legs, which were wrapped tightly around his waist, fell limp against him.

Finn grabbed a fistful of her hair and pulled her head to the side. He whispered in her ear, "He was a fool to let you go."

He zipped his jeans, planted a hard kiss on her lips and left her standing there, practically naked as he closed the door softly behind him.

Farrah dropped to her knees and sobbed. The handsome Irishman left her body satiated, and her soul ripped to shreds.

***

How could a perfect stranger recognize her value, and Aaron, the man she'd given everything to for years, discard her without even so much as a goodbye?

God she hated him. And he would pay. Or, was the all-knowing Irishman right when he said she wanted her ex back?

"There's a thin line between love and hate, Farrah Jane," he said, moving his hand up to encircle her waist.

It didn't help that he was helping her blur that line so wickedly.

TABLE OF CONTENTS

Chapter 1

"You hired an escort? You're paying some guy to go to your ex-fiance's wedding with you? You have truly lost it," Farrah's best friend, Priscilla, said.

"He's not an escort," Farrah corrected.

"Then why are you paying him? And you know Aaron will see right through your little ploy. He knows you like a book."

"I'm not paying him. I'm paying *for* him to accompany me; that's all. I invited him, so of course I'm picking up the tab. It's proper etiquette. That's the way we were raised, remember?"

"What does he do for a living that he can't afford to take a weekend trip, even if you did do the inviting? He's a man. Men pay their own way. *That's* proper etiquette."

"I met him last night and took him home and fucked his brains out. I asked him to pretend to be my lover. That's why he's going," Farrah screamed into the phone. "There. That's the situation. Are you happy?!"

The truth was, the Irishman had fucked her brains out. Or, they'd fucked each other's brains out. Whatever. It didn't matter, Farrah concluded. A lot of fucking had gone on, as her jumping center reminded her. Just the thought of what she'd experienced in the arms of the handsome stranger she'd woken to had her needing a maxi pad to stem the flow of juices.

Their mating had been vicious, savage, barbaric … and beautiful. And she wanted more of it. Of him. Much more.

Even Aaron, the man she'd loved for almost a decade, had never veered close to making her come like the stranger from the bar last night. It made him the perfect man to show up with to her ex-fiance's wedding.

Aaron would be able to smell another man's cock on her, and feel how much she enjoyed it. She knew he would because the kind of mind-blowing sex she'd experienced last night didn't stay confined to the bedroom. It seeped out of your pores and brought a stupid grin to your face for the world to see, crave and wonder about.

"Farrah you're not serious? Please tell me you're joking just to get me to shut up," Priscilla said.

"I'm not, and it's no big deal. It was just sex. Great sex. And there's nothing wrong with that," Farrah defended, wondering why she was still friends with Priscilla. Their friendship was more of a force of habit than a real relationship she was coming to believe; like a lot of shit in her life. When you start from the same place, it makes sense. But she and Priscilla had long since grown apart.

They were no longer debutantes who went to the same private school; belonged to the same country clubs; and went off to the same Ivy-league college – but not for an education. The reason young women and like she and Priscilla went to university was to land a husband capable of keeping them in the style to which they'd been raised. It was nineteenth-century thinking in the twenty-first century; a testament that time didn't change much in certain circles.

Princess Diana had found that out the hard way. One could say she died trying to run away from the confines of an old-world system that didn't support the new-world happiness she craved. Almost a quarter of a century after her death, her daughter-in-law, Meghan Markle, was learning the same hard lesson. Farrah sighed as her mind made the comparison.

Priscilla had followed the old-world script, almost to perfection. She had landed said rich husband – even though he was almost thirty years older than her and made her vagina drier than the Mojave desert. The reason Farrah knew this is because Priscilla had blurted it out over one too many Grey Goose vodka jello shots at her bachelorette party. It was the only time Priscilla's mask ever slipped – when she drank too much.

***

"You don't have to go through with this marriage, you know. You can still say no," Farrah said.

"No I can't," Priscilla returned, her face stone-cold sober for a few seconds. "I'm not like you Farrah. I've never had to worry about anything, especially money. And I like it that way."

"Wow," was all Farrah could think to reply. "Are you sure Priscilla?"

"Damn sure!" Priscilla laughed, the alcohol seeping back into her gaze. "For one, my parents would kill me if I didn't after the fortune they've spent on this wedding. And two," she said, loopily holding up two fingers, "you can always fuck the pool boy when you get tired of faking it with Mr. Limp Dick."

Farrah's breath caught in her throat.

Priscilla looked at her and let out a peel of giggles. "Don't look so shocked Farrah.

Maybe after a dose of trying to make it in the cold, hard world, you'll be next in the bridal line."

***

Although, like Priscilla, Farrah had never had to worry about money, she knew that she could never marry just for the sake of it. It had to be all-in love, or nothing.

After university, she had done the unthinkable gone the other direction. She put her marketing degree to use, instead of settling on a rich husband. She was the vice president of sales at a digital marketing agency, one of the fastest-expanding tech companies in the country. She loved her job. The independence it afforded her gave her a sense of value – something she had struggled all her life to feel.

And, that's where she'd met the love of her life – Aaron. She had thought he felt the same – until five months ago when he'd left her. And now, he was getting married to someone else.

A man who had told her that he didn't believe in marriage.

Who had said he was married to his career.

Who had said that she, Farrah, was the only woman he'd ever want to marry, if he believed in marriage.

Aaron had given her an engagement ring after she admitted over one too many glasses of wine one night that she really did want to get married. It seemed that in the last two years, all of her friends were getting married.

They'd just come from yet another wedding. That made five in nineteen months – three of which she'd been a bridesmaid in. *Always a bridesmaid and never a bride.* The innocent joke by a casual acquaintance at the reception had finally taken a toll on her heart. The wine unlocked a torrent of tears, and she'd admitted to Aaron that she did want to get married.

A week later, Aaron had surprised Farrah with an engagement ring. He hadn't exactly asked her to marry him. Farrah didn't realize that until later because she'd been so caught up in the excitement of actually getting a ring. Upon placing it on her finger, he said, *'I hope this allays any fears you have about my commitment to you."*

Farrah had tearfully nodded her head, the three-carat, pear-cut sparkler blooming her heart with hope that if he could take this step, he'd eventually warm up to having children as well. For almost a decade of her life – two years as his fiance – she'd hung in there with him; given him her heart and soul. She had loved him – and still did – that much.

But he'd left her.

Farrah came home to their apartment one day, and he was just … gone. Although the apartment looked the same, she felt in her bones that something was different. The tightness in her chest signaled it. The negative energy suffocated her.

It wasn't until she looked in the closet and saw only her things that she knew for sure that the feeling in her chest wasn't just a panic attack; her anxiety acting up.

To this day, she still didn't know how her being had known something was off. But she had. The why of it had ceased to matter. Only the fact that he was gone did. For good. And here she was almost six months later, still trying to pick up the pieces.

Priscilla's droning voice snatched Farrah back to the present.

"Are you willing to pay the price for this so-called great sex, Farrah? An orgasm is an orgasm. You don't have to sacrifice your dignity to get one. It's like I don't even know you anymore. Ever since you and Aaron broke up, you've become little more than a ... well a common, loose woman. You need to get control of yourself; get control of your life."

Farrah's mouth became the loose cannon she'd been conditioned to control since the day she was born. Now it was time for a few cannonballs to fly, and this bitch had just given her the ammo she needed to fire away.

"Let's set the record straight. I haven't had sex with anyone since Aaron until last night. No one! I may have mistakenly rushed back into the dating game, but no one has put his dick in my pussy. And speaking of dicks in pussies, I'm willing to bet you your newest Fendi bag that that limp-dick husband of yours hasn't given you an orgasm since … never! I'll bet your hair is as perfect when you finish fucking him as when you start. So you can shove your worthless opinion up that tight ass of yours and go straight to hell!"

Farrah angrily jabbed at the disconnect button her her phone, wishing for once that rotary phones were still in use so she could slam the receiver down. Somehow, punching at a button didn't give the same satisfaction as slamming down a fat, fistful of receiver.

One so-called best friend down, and anyone-else-who-dared-cross-her-path-today to go. She was tired of living her life by the rules of the little bubble she had lived and grown up in on the Upper East Side of New York City.

In a city of over eight and a half million people, the world of the upper crust could be surprisingly – and suffocatingly – small. Even though she'd been raised in it, Farrah had never felt comfortable. The adopted black daughter of a white, English father and a black American mother, she had been accepted, but only because of who her parents were; not because of who she was. At least, that's the way she had always felt.

Priscilla had become her 'bestie' in fifth grade. But Farrah had always felt like some kind of token black friend. Over the last twenty years, she could recall hundreds of barbs, innuendos, conversations and situations that reinforced that feeling. But she'd never rebelled; never made a fuss; never acted anything less than the attractive, cultured young woman she was raised to be.

And look what it had gotten her. A resentful attitude and a broken heart;

one that wouldn't heal no matter how much effort she put into it. In the last six months, she'd been in a frenzy to get past her hurt; to get over Aaron.

She'd gone to a therapist.

She'd tried meditation.

She'd even gone on a ten-day, 'change your life' retreat in the jungle in South America. One anaconda; two long-ass centipedes; a few thousand mosquito bites; and a few bigger-than-any-spider-should-ever-be sightings later, and she'd decided she could live with heartbreak. It was just the way things were going to be because nothing or no one had been able to shake Aaron or the constant thoughts of him from her heart.

Until last night.

Chapter 2

Last Night

The first touch of his lips showered her in a kaleidoscope of exploding color.

This stranger – the softness of his lips; the perfect bow of them, which were almost girlish; his expert manipulation of her tongue with his – knew her kissing language. He kissed her like his lips had been made expressly for the purpose of one day meeting hers. She wanted to go on kissing him forever.

They kissed until the bar closed, and on the side of every building between the establishment and her condo six blocks away. They couldn't go ten steps without their lips devouring each other.

Farrah knew that if he pulled her into an alley to fuck her on the side of one of those buildings, she wouldn't have resisted.

They barely made it inside her apartment fully clothed.

***

His lips circled her clit, then suctioned themselves onto the jumping bud.

Farrah buried her hands in the thickness of his hair, circling her hips as his tongue performed a magical dance between her legs.

"Just like that baby. Oh god just like that. Suck me. Suck me!" she commanded as her hips gyrated into a mamba.

His tongue slid down the sleek line of her vagina, delving into the slippery depths as one finger slid in.

Tongue. Suction. Circle clit.

Finger. Slide in. Slide out. Rub clit.

Tongue. Suction. Circle clit.

Finger. Slide in. Slide out. Rub clit.

The expert timing and orchestration gave Farrah's head the spins. She felt the rumbling of an on-coming explosion, then he withdrew everything. Tongue. Lips. Fingers. Everything.

Farrah's eyes flew open at the interruption of nirvana.

He smiled a devilish smile, the light from the one window in her bedroom making him look almost sinister. A menacing sex god she wanted to drown herself in from now til forever.

"I'm not going anywhere," he said at her wild look and unspoken question.

Farrah nodded her head and yanked at his belt. She whimpered in anticipation and frustration as she tried to unbuckle it.

He smiled at her eagerness, his hands on his hips as he admired her bobbing breasts and the smooth sheen of sweat on her skin.

His belt successfully unbuckled, Farrah prepared to yank his underwear down. To her surprise and delight, he wasn't wearing any. His cock sprang free – long, hard, swollen and … beautiful.

He grabbed a fistful of her hair and yanked her head back, the length of his steel-hard member brushing warmly against the softness of her lips. Before he had time to ask or hope, Farrah greedily took the rock-hard length of it into her mouth. Her jaw opened wide and warm, drawing him deep into the back of her throat. Her mouth watered from the intrusion of the delicious taste and feel of him.

Finn growled at the expert veracity of her tongue as she guided him in and out of her mouth. It was almost like a mold prepared specifically for his swollen staff.

He breathed heavily, his hands tightening in her hair as she moved her head back and forth. Then faster. She could sense, rather than see, the concave contraction of his flat stomach as he wrestled to maintain the control she was close to ripping away from him.

"Woman," he said, expelling a low growl. He pushed her away from him and onto her back. He bent over her, breathing hard into her face as she looked into his eyes. He slid his hands between her legs, thrusting his fingers in her again. It was almost like he'd taken personal lessons on how to navigate her pulsing vagina.

She could feel his shaft pulsing against her slick thigh. He removed his fingers form her and slid his length up and down the soaked slope of her sleek walls. Her center throbbed. Her everything throbbed.

"If you don't want this woman, speak now or forever hold your peace."

Woman. How did he know she liked to be called that?

"Now," she said simply.

He looked at her as if he couldn't believe the seductress before him, his staff pulsing as Farrah laid on her back and spread her legs for him. Her beautiful, wet, soaked, pink pussy offered up on a silver platter.

He leaned over her, lifted her smooth, tight ass and slammed his cock home.

Farrah screamed in pleasure and pain, shocked by the fullness as he stretched her to fit him.

He could feel her clinch around him, pushing at his chest as she straddled the line between pleasure and pain.

"It's ok. It's ok," he whispered in her ear as he slowed his movements, sensing her discomfort.

His lips traced a trail from her earlobe to the center of her throat. He waited for her to start moving under him, signaling that she was ready for the full length of him again.

He eased slowly and deeper into her wetness, whispering words Farrah only marginally caught as she allowed herself to be transported to that supernatural place between lovers.

"Perfection," he whispered, saying her name over and over in his deep, Irish lilt. The sound of his voice and the feel of him inside her ignited an inferno.

Farrah couldn't hold back any longer. Her body jack-knifed beneath him as she crashed headlong into her orgasm. "Rip that pussy baby! Tear that shit up!" she said, the heat inside her making her lose any sort of decorum or control as she hissed and twisted under him.

He held on, a fist of her hair in his hands as he plunged into her again and again.

Farrah locked her legs around him, and sank her teeth into the corded muscle of his shoulder. "Fuck me baby. Dear god yes fuck me!" she yelled as her body careened into the sea of bliss that had been waiting for her since they met – a mere two hours ago.

***

"I didn't know I was in a for a ride quite like that," Finn said, staring at the ceiling as he waited for his breathing to become even once again.

"Why, don't I look like I'm good in bed?"

It occurred to him that he hadn't fucked her at all. But she'd fucked the shit out of him! Her pussy was so good it had to be literally designed and chiseled to life by God himself.

"Not like that," he said, turning to look at her. "If any woman looked like she could fuck like that, she wouldn't make it down the street safely everyday."

Farrah laughed.

"You're a beautiful woman, especially when you laugh," he said, admiring her perfect white teeth, smooth skin and halo of hair.

"And you're a beautiful man, especially when you're inside me," Farrah said lasciviously.

"Then I must not disappoint," he said, and flipped her over on her side. This time, he was going to be the one doing the fucking.

He fleetingly thought of his last lover, and how she had always gave him a run for his money between the sheets. Be he'd always been in control. As he eased inside Farrah from behind, all the muscles in his body quivered in anticipation of the pleasure to come – and just how easily she could wrest control from him; something it had never occurred to him was possible.

After the first thrust, he stilled himself at the sinful tightness of her. *Concentrate,* he admonished himself, determined to stay in control.

"Hmmm," Farrah moaned, as she eased her tight little ass back into him.

"I could bury myself in you all night long," he whispered as concentrated on easing into her again inch by sinfully, feel-good inch.

"May daylight never come," Farrah said as she ran one hand along his balls.

He gave himself over to the exquisite tightness of her heated center, as the night bearing witness to the perfect explosion of their passion.

Chapter 3

Farrah stared at the stranger in her bed.

Aaron who? It was the first night in almost six months that she hadn't thought about, dreamed about, or cried about her ex.

"Do you always look so serious in the morning? Quite the difference from last night," the heavenly beautiful one said. His perfect teeth – and eyes, and nose, and chest and everything else, was on full on display. His beauty was provocative. And exciting.

"Are you always so nosy in the morning? Quite the difference from last night," Farrah snapped.

He stared at her for a few seconds. In a way he appreciated her clipped response. It put control firmly back in his court, because he'd lost it last night, and at the first look at her face this morning, he wasn't sure if he could get it back. She was even more beautiful in the broad light of day.

Losing control; that was foreign territory. This – snideness – he could deal with. He got up, picked his jeans up from the floor on her side of the bed, and proceeded to put them on.

"Where are you going?" Farrah asked.

"Last night was nice. Very nice," he smiled. "But I know when it's time to leave."

Farrah noted that there was no sarcasm in his voice. No anger. No nothing. Just calmness. "I … I don't want you to leave," she stammered, trying to harness her emotions, which were as scattered as a dropped bag of marbles.

He looked at her, taking in her swollen, 'fuck me again lips' and innocent, Sunday-school-girl eyes. The message was so clearly delivered that he fought the urge to forget how easily she had made him lose himself in her last night, and climb back in bed with her. She was a mass of contradiction that messed with his psyche. No woman had ever done that. No woman would ever be allowed to do that. *But this one could*, his subconscious alerted.

"That beautiful mouth of yours says one thing, but your attitude says another. I'm a big fan of following actions instead of believing words," he said, so serenely that they might have been discussing the weather.

How could he be so philosophical so early in the morning? "I-- dammit," Farrah said, balling a fistful of sheet in her hands.

She caught sight of the clock on her nightstand: 9:30. It wasn't so early after all. She never slept this late. Ever. Not even on vacation, which is what she was on right now. Instead of jetting off to some foreign land, she'd decided to stay home; have a stay-cation. New York City was perfect for that.

She'd once dated a guy who had proudly proclaimed that he'd never left the island of Manhattan. While that had creeped her out, she understood on some level how it could happen. The city offered everything one could ever want.

The solid rock of handsomeness before her was in the middle of covering all his gorgeousness.

Farrah peered at the clock again. Maybe she was cranky because she hadn't gotten her morning run in. By this time of morning, she'd completed a three-mile jog in Central Park, had breakfast and been at work for a couple of hours.

Farrah shook her head. Whatever the reason, she still couldn't quite believe that she was in bed at this hour.

The gorgeous one was pulling his white t-shirt over his head. It wasn't quite form fitting. But, it was snug enough that Farrah could see the defined lines of his broad chest and flat stomach.

"Something wrong?" he asked at her confused look. "I happen to be a very good listener," he said, pulling on some stylish black leather ankle boots. They reminded Farrah of motorcycle boots. Very East Village. Very masculine. Very him.

Farrah found herself wondering what he did for a living. All of a sudden, she was a little ashamed that beyond his name – his first name; Finn – she knew absolutely nothing about him. She could have had sex with a serial killer last night for all she knew.

Maybe Priscilla was right. Maybe she should get ahold of herself a little better. Bringing a stranger home wasn't exactly the smartest way to be living.

But then, almost six months of pent-up hurt gushing out of you wasn't exactly conducive to being smart either.

"Good listener? Hmmm … that would make you an anomaly in the male kingdom," Farrah replied, burying her head in her hands to stop the sudden tears that pricked her eyes.

Not now. God please not now, she prayed in those few seconds.

"So I've been told," he chuckled. "But listening is an art form; one I found early on that I quite enjoy. So give it a whirl. What's wrangling you?"

Farrah laughed. "Wrangling? That's funny."

"I'm glad I amuse you," he said.

"I am too," Farrah said.

"Why?" he returned, sitting on the bed beside her.

Farrah could feel his breath on her face. Desire slid in where humor resided seconds ago. She felt the moistness between her legs. Her heart galloped in her chest; her mouth a sudden patch of the Sahara in its dryness.

"I ... I ..."

"Do I make you nervous, little one?" Finn said, brushing her right cheek with his left hand.

Farrah raised her lashes to him. "No. You don't make me nervous at all," she admitted. For any number of reasons – stranger, gorgeous, intense – he should have made her more than nervous. But the truth was, she'd never felt so at ease with a stranger. The way she'd responded to him last night underscored this.

Why? she thought.

Finn rubbed the padding of his thumb across her bottom lip. His other hand kneaded the back of her neck.

A swath of brownish-black curls hung over his arm as they stared at each other. For a few seconds, Farrah felt the calmness of simply being. Breathing felt like expelling miniature clouds.

"You're jumpy," he laughed as the alarm on his watch broke the spell between them.

"No I'm not. Anyone would have jumped in that situation," Farrah snapped, as he turned the offending sound off.

"Are you always so cranky in the mornings? I've heard of such people," he said, as she held her hand over her chest.

"Such people?" Farrah said, her eyebrows searching for her hairline. "Now I'm reduced to being 'a people?'" she said, putting air quotes around the offending phrase.

"We're all people. Why does that offend you? Or is it just I who offends you?" Finn replied.

"You know what offends me Mr. Mr...."

"The name is Finn, remember? And I'd take a gander and say that just about everything offends you. Are you upset about the way you responded to me last night? Embarrassed by your, shall we say, very lively performance? Is that what this is all about? Because for the life of me woman, I can't imagine what the hell you're so miffed about this early in the morning," he finished, losing his customary cool.

"Number one, it is not early," Farrah shot back. "And number two, stop using words like miffed and wrangled and gander. Nobody talks like that!

And number three--"

"Are you calling me a nobody?" Finn said, cutting off her tirade. "Would you like me to prove to you again just what a somebody I am? Maybe it'll put the sugar back where the vinegar has obviously spilled," he said, leaning into her as he grabbed her by the back of the neck again.

Farrah could see the mirth in the ocean-blue depths of his eyes. No eyes had a right to be that blue. As blue as the Caribbean sea, with the same depth of ever-changing color.

"I really should hate you for talking to me like that," Farrah said, grabbing ahold of his forearm as she leaned her forehead into his.

"Like what?" he said slowly, wrestling with the smile that wanted to split his too-beautiful lips. "I know in this age of fake news telling the truth is somewhat of an anomaly. But, I gave you more credit."

"For what? And why?" Farrah asked, surprised that by how much she relished his compliment. Aaron almost never gave her straightforward compliments. Somehow, they were always back-handed or a little off.

"Because last night you told me the truth," Finn responded.

"I don't remember us doing much talking last night," Farrah said, blushing. She hadn't blushed this much in the almost ten years she'd known Aaron, she thought.

Stop thinking about him! her brain screamed.

"While it is true that very few words passed our lips, we did have quite the conversation last evening. Communication takes many forms. And you have quite the unique way of communicating, little one."

Farrah lowered her lids. Their bodies did seem to have a language of their own.

Finn put a finger under her chin to lift her gaze to his again. "And this, I think, is what has you on edge this morning. ... All the more reason I should take my leave. And for the record, you have nothing to be embarrassed about," he said, the desire in her eyes making him turn away from her.

"No," the word rushed out of Farrah before she could contain it. She tightened her grip on his forearm. "I ... it's ... I never sleep this late. And I haven't had my coffee. I'm just feeling a little out of sorts," she explained.

"You know what they say about good sex? It's better than any sleeping pill," he chuckled at the question in her eyes.

Farrah blushed, yet again, as she took in the rumpled sheets on her bed. The top one was half-way off. She gathered it to her, covering her nakedness more fully. "I'm sorry," she said, all of a sudden very shy and wanting to change the subject to anything other than what had transpired between them last night. *Who was that woman,* she wondered. She'd behaved like a sex-starved whore. And she'd loved every second of it. "I didn't mean to snap at you."

"Apology accepted. Now would you like to talk about what the real issue is? As I said, I'm a very good listener."

That Irish lilt. Damn he was sexy as hell! Farrah had never seen a more beautiful man. Not even Aaron, who no man had ever been able to live up to for her. Every since the day she'd laid eyes on him, her eyes – and heart, and entire being had been his and his alone.

But this stranger penetrated that bubble. He occupied a tiny piece of the rarefied space that only Aaron had existed in. And, after only one night. The reality disturbed her.

"Why would you want to listen to the problems of a complete stranger?"

"We're strangers, but I wouldn't say complete strangers. Not after last night," Finn smiled, remembering the tightness of her God-chiseled pussy. It's the way he would always think of it – and her. She was perfection in a female. Definitely God-hewn.

Another damn blush! Jesus! she thought.

She couldn't believe the way she'd given herself to him and talked to him last night. Maybe it was because he was a stranger. There were no expectations. No rules. No 'after' to be worried about. It was just complete, unadulterated, raw fucking. And she hadn't had that in so long. Or really, never, she realized.

She thought she and Aaron had had an amazing sex life, until last night. She would never have behaved that way with him. He would have thought it uncivilized; even dirty on some level. It was definitely not the way a fiance or wife should behave.

But Finn hadn't seemed to mind – at all. He'd fucked her practically into rawness, slamming into her so many times she was sure her vagina was now molded to the shape of his perfectly sculpted cock.

"Why did you come home with me last night?" Farrah asked, frustrated with her line of thinking, and simultaneously excited at the way her vagina started to pulse. "Is it something you do all the time?"

With his looks, she imagined he could go home with a different woman every night of the week if he wanted. Hell, several women a night! He was just that beautiful. There was an earthy, chiseled beauty to him, overlaid with distinctively feminine features; like his ridiculously long eyelashes and heart-shaped, pink lips. It was a fascinating juxtaposition that was impossible to resist. No woman could keep her panties on in his presence, Farrah justified to herself.

"One night stands are not my thing," Finn smiled. And in spite of that wicked little smile, Farrah believed him. Something in her core told her it was true.

"Why me?" Farrah pressed, curious.

It was a good question, because he didn't do one night stands. It really wasn't his thing. His art had been the only *lady* in his life for a long time. And she was no one night stand. She was a lifetime commitment; one that no woman could replace.

His thoughts strayed to his last lover. She was beautiful in the classic sense. Long, blonde hair; legs for days; a waist his hand could span, and perfectly formed breasts that always invited his lips. Her green eyes could go from a cold jade to a burning emerald in no time; at times the color reminding him of so many things about his homeland of Ireland, which he missed mightily.

New York was one hell of an expensive city, and a night out could easily cost a couple of hundred bucks. He just didn't have that kind of money. So he never let himself get close to anyone, especially a woman. Luckily, that was easy in New York. It was made for the unattached; filled with the ambitious who had no time or need for love. While many women liked the idea of an artist as a boyfriend or lover, they had little patience for the broke reality of said artist.

Women in his age bracket were at a stage in life where they were looking for a suitable mate for marriage and children, which meant financial stability – and Finn was anything but.

He worked all the time, but he was far from financially secure. And if he wasn't working, he was thinking about work. So he'd bed them, and they'd quickly fade away when he couldn't afford the latest weekend in the Hamptons or ticket to the Met. Sometimes he was convinced that he only had the lust gene because it was always easy to let them – whoever the them 'she' was at the moment – go. He hadn't felt a real connection to anyone in the six years he'd been in New York.

Until her. His latest lover. She'd been different.

An art lover, she understood his work; in fact, was fascinated by it. He had longed for that kind of connection with a woman. A woman who could separate the work from the man; yet know when to fuse the two.

This woman had intrinsically understood that – and so much more. She'd even had the connections to help him with his career, which he hadn't known about until the agent known for making careers had called him out of the blue one day.

***

"She was right, you could be the next Warhol or Basquiat," the gangly agent said.

"My work is nothing like either," Finn replied, wondering if he'd made a mistake taking a meeting with the agent his lover had practically insisted on.

"Of course not. I was referring to their fame. Your work is unique. And with your looks; it's a match made in art heaven. You're going to be quite the hit. I hope you're ready for all that's coming your way: the fame, the opportunity, the money. The world is about to become your oyster, Mr. O'Hare. And I've seen that destroy many a talented artist. Basquiat is perhaps one of the more famous examples. So talented; such a waste. The things he could have done."

This is the side of being an artist Finn hated. He didn't want to be the next anybody. He just wanted to make good art, and have it appreciated. Maybe he should have stayed anonymous. He must have voiced the sentiment aloud, because the agent recoiled almost in horror.

"Are you kidding me? With a face and body like that? I hate to break it to you Mr. O'Hare, but the thing that's going to get you noticed is not your work — as fabulous as it is — at least not initially. What's going to get you noticed is 'this,' his agent said, running a hand up and down the front of him."

Finn simply stared at the man before him, trying to decide if this was the right move for his career. He was very uncomfortable with what the agent was saying. It was almost like he had to be some kind of superficial front for his own work.

"I don't normally represent unknowns," the agent said, breaking into his thoughts. "But lucky for you, I recognize talent. And I recognize what can get said talent from A to Z. This," he said again, referring to Finn's physical beauty, "is it. And when you throw in the melody of your Irish lilt — and your raw talent — you're going to explode on the scene."

"The fact that you put my art last--" Finn said, on the verge of saying no. This was all wrong.

"Have you not been listening to a thing I've said?" the agent insisted. "It is the last thing people are interested in — at first. You must understand this."

Finn grimaced.

"If you want me to represent you, trust me, your art will be what you're known for — eventually. But you are the delicious bait on the hook. Once I reel them in, your art will speak for itself. You have to trust me Finn," the agent said. "Otherwise, I can't represent you. You're the artist. I would never tell you how to do your work. But I'm also an artist … at what I do. Don't let the pomp and circumstance fool you. I am the best for a reason," the agent said, with no trace of cockiness.

Finn looked at his hot pink boa, black beret, black boots, dark-navy jeans and black cashmere sweater. He was flashy. The hot-pink boa screamed flamboyance. But the rest of his ensemble was sensible, Finn reasoned. Remove the boa, and it was an ensemble he himself would wear. And the agent had come highly recommended. Word was, he made stars; not that Finn cared about that. But he did long to make a living from his work.

He knew his work was good. And he'd been trying for almost six years to get his career off the ground in New York. But his visa was about to expire and if he couldn't make a go of it now, he'd have to go back to that little seaside town in Ireland where he had a practically nil chance of getting an opportunity like this again.

"Alright, you have yourself a deal," Finn said, shaking the agent's hand, sincerely hoping that he wasn't making a mistake.

***

After that meeting, he'd seen a change in his lover. She'd become more demanding; almost obsessive, treating him like he owed her something. He'd worked too hard and too long to have his success usurped by someone else's efforts.

The more she acted like he owed her something, the more evident it had become that there was no future for them. While he hadn't been in love, he could have seen maybe getting there one day with her. But it was not to be. He ended their relationship.

And, that's what had driven him to that little hole-in-the-wall Irish bar in midtown Manhattan last night. He had been intent on drowning his sorrows amongst some of his fellow countrymen.

You could always find an Irishman in an Irish bar in New York City. A real Irishman; one from the motherland. Only, that's not what he'd found at all. He'd found something much better.

Whiskey and friends hadn't been his cure. He'd known that they wouldn't be as soon as he'd spotted Farrah sitting at the bar. He had watched her for a good five minutes to make sure she was alone before having the bartender send a drink over.

She had looked over at him, held the glass up in salute, and downed the shot of Bushmills, single malt whiskey in one swallow – the way a shot of good whiskey should be drank, he'd smiled to her across the bar.

Her perfect lips had puckered as she swallowed, and he had known from that second that he had to have her. He'd already imagined her lips sealed around his cock, and he wanted to bury himself in what he knew would be her velvety depths.

***

"Why did I come home with you?" he repeated Farrah's question, cupping his chin in concentration. The move made him look so damned handsome standing there at the end of her bed that Farrah almost jumped up and pulled him back down with her.

The longer he took to answer, the more curious she was. Was there a wife? A girlfriend? Was he cheating, and trying to figure out whether to tell her the truth or not?

"To paraphrase an old Irish saying, 'There are only two kinds of men in the world, the Irish and those who wish they were.' You looked like you could use a bit of Irish charm last night," he said.

"Not stuck on yourself at all, are you?" Farrah said, throwing a pillow at him.

"Not at all," he smiled, catching the pillow and tossing it back to her.

God he was gorgeous!

"Seriously?" Farrah said.

"Alright. Seriously. I came home with you because I wanted you. And evidently, you felt the same," he smiled.

Farrah pursed her lips and looked away in embarrassment.

"Really. It's that simple, huh?" she asked.

"Men tend to be amazingly simple creatures – for better or worse," he said, those azure eyes searing her, making her juices flow faster.

"So there's no wife. No girlfriend. No current or ex anybody? You don't have to lie to me, you know? Consider this the freebie fuck that shall remain a secret. Everyone is entitled to at least one of those in their lifetime."

"Do you really believe that?" he asked.

"Believe what?" Farrah asked innocently.

"That everyone is entitled to cheat at least once?"

"No," Farrah said truthfully, feeling chastened and not sure why. She didn't want him to think ill of her, even though they'd just met.

"I just didn't want you to feel awkward telling me the truth about a wife or girlfriend," she explained.

"There is no wife or girlfriend. I came home with you because I desired you. That's the truth, the whole truth, and nothing but the truth," he said, crossing his arms over his chest.

Damn if he doesn't look like an LL Bean or Calvin Klein ad, Farrah thought, biting down on her bottom lip and crossing her arms tightly over her chest to keep from pouncing on him. She could sense he was ready to go, and she wasn't ready to let him go. Not yet. *Not anytime soon*, a silent voice insisted.

Farrah ignored it, but she did want to keep him talking. "Are you always so easy going? So unassuming?"

"How do you say here in America … what you see is what you get."

"What is your last name?"

He laughed out loud at that. "I guess we did kinda put the cart before the horse, didn't we?" he observed. He came to stand beside the bed instead of at the foot of it, and extended a hand. "I'm Finneas O'Hare."

Farrah smiled and took it. "Nice to officially meet you Finneas O'Hare. I'm Farrah Jane Bryant."

"Farrah … like *Charlie's Angels* Farrah?"

"Yep," Farrah said. "Only, obviously I'm no blonde bombshell."

"No you're not. But you're every bit as beautiful," he said, looking at her full breasts pressed tightly against the sheet she had tucked under her arms. He remembered the silky-softness of them in his hands. The smooth roughness of her aroused nipples. He felt his dick getting hard.

"Sweet talker," Farrah said.

"We Irish do have a way with the ladies," he said. "But now sweet Farrah Jane, it's time to take my leave."

"No, Finneas," Farrah objected. "Not if you don't have to. I'd like to know more about you. Can you stay for a while; talk some more?" she said, an idea forming in her head.

He'd be absolutely perfect. Almost too perfect, she thought, chewing on her bottom lip as she tried to talk herself into dismissing the crazy, just-forming idea.

"Only my mother calls me Finneas; friends call me Finn."

Farrah smiled. "Alright, Finn. Can you stay for a while? I'll even make you coffee."

"Coffee. What, no breakfast after all of that activity last night?" he teased. "I'm starved."

"I don't cook," Farrah admitted almost sheepishly. "At all. I hate it – so I don't do it. But I'd be happy to order something in. And there's fruit and yogurt."

Finn laughed. "A woman who doesn't cook. To an Irishman, that's almost a cardinal sin."

"To a lot of men," Farrah laughed. "Maybe that's why I'm still single," she said, wrapping the sheet tighter around her as she struggled to get out of bed. "So that means you'll stay for a while?"

Finn looked at his watch, thinking about the meeting he had later that day. A meeting that could make or break the trajectory of his life.

"I can stay. And how 'bout I make coffee, and see what else I can rustle up. I refuse to believe that your cubbards are as bare as you say."

"Great," Farrah said. "Knock yourself out. I'm just going to hop in the shower right quick."

Finn pointed at the sheet wrapped around her. "Why so shy? I know every curve," he said, his tongue peeping out to swab his bottom lip.

Farrah felt her center steaming.

Standing there in jeans and boots and a white t-shirt – her favorite outfit of all time on any man – and with that devilish smile, she almost said the hell with a shower.

"Not every curve," she said.

He closed the distance between them.

"Every curve, Farrah Jane," he said, picking her up and laying her back down on the bed to prove his point.

***

He buried himself deep inside her, and she began the slow, teasing rotation of her hips that tested his control.

She grabbed his face between her hands. "I want to see you when you're inside me," she commanded.

He chuckled at that, "Your wish is my command," he said, palming her smooth, naked ass as he inched his way deeper. He loved her take-charge attitude in the bedroom, even though how easily she bewitched him gave him pause. A woman who actually enjoyed sex for sex sake; not as some kind of power play. They existed, he smiled as he stroked deeper into her.

Her pussy felt warm and soft, like a delicious, freshly backed custard. It enveloped him, suctioning his cock as if it wanted to squeeze the very life from him. She must do kegel, because her pussy walls contracted so tightly around him, it was almost like she was milking him.

"Hold on," he growled as she tightened around him again.

Farrah smiled, enjoying the control she had over him. She knew she could make him come any time she wanted. She squeezed again. He reached into the pit of the last bit of control he had to keep from coming.

"You naughty little bitch," he grunted, his body convulsing in rigid spasms as he fought off release. Being inside her – a perfect stranger – he felt home. This new feeling excited and worried him at the same time.

"Fuck me, Finn. Fuck me harder, baby," Farrah grunted as he stared at her in awe.

Maybe she was some kind of voodoo princess, he thought, because her pussy put a spell on his cock that was hard to control. And he was always in control of his dick.

Always.

With one more wicked turn of her fantastic hips, he lost the control he had never had to fight for before.

"God damn woman," he said as his body jerked and shuddered in climax. He pulled out of her, the condom halfway down his staff.

"What?" Farrah said, as he stared at her.

"You are a wicked, wicked woman Farrah Jane," he said, pulling the condom completely off.

"You have no idea," Farrah said, her plan completely formulated.

"I think I called you a bitch," he confessed. "I'm sorry about that."

"I'm not," Farrah said. "Passion has its own language, and in that moment, I wanted to be the hot bitch you were fucking."

Finn shook his head. This woman was going to have him behaving like a bobblehead she was so full of contractions.

He had never called a woman the "B" word in his life; not even in anger. It just wasn't his style of relating. But this woman – she took him out of himself. Classy on the outside, and just whorish enough on the inside to be hella dangerous. Sweet Jesus, she was perfection! He knew that as long as he lived, he would forever dream about making love to this woman – no matter who it was he was making love to at the time.

He looked over at her, obviously deep in thought. About what, he'd give his soul to know.

***

Yes, he was perfect, for this ... and so much else, Farrah thought. She turned to him. "Got another one of those?" she asked, pointing to the condom.

His grin was sinful, as sinful as she felt as he slid his tongue over an already engorged nipple.

Chapter 4

"So you want me to go to your ex-fiance's wedding with you, and pretend to be your boyfriend?"

"No. I want you to pretend to be my lover. But really, it's not pretending because right now, you are my lover."

"Where I come from, a lover is much more. This is just sex. Great sex, but just sex, nevertheless." As he said the words, they didn't feel right. They felt inadequate. *Untrue,* he thought, surprised at the feeling.

"Let's work with my definition," Farrah said. She didn't want to be more to him. *She didn't,* she responded to the tiny piece of her that for some strange reason resisted. He was heartbreak attached to a fabulous piece of dick. And she'd had enough of heartbreak to last her a lifetime. But what she hadn't had enough of for almost half a year was dick – fabulous or otherwise. And as long as he was around, she planned to get as much of that as she could – and get revenge on her ex.

"Tell me about this man who left you; who has you so set on revenge. You should be thanking his wife-to-be, by the way," Finn said, as she traced circles on his chest.

"How do you know he left me? And what in God's name do I have to thank the woman who took my place for?" Farrah sulked.

"The fact that you're plotting revenge is a dead giveaway that he left you. Otherwise, you wouldn't be picking up strange men in bars, bringing them home and trying to fuck their brains out," he teased, wanting to take the sting out of his words. "It worked out great for me, but you don't strike me as the kind of woman who does that on a regular basis. As for thanking his wife to be – if he left you, he's obviously a fool. No woman wants a fool for a husband. Trust me, she did you a favor. You owe her a big thank you for the fifteen or twenty years you would have spent finding that out."

"You presume a lot," she said slowly. "He's actually a pretty great guy," Farrah said sadly, as she continued to trace circles on his chest. His skin was so smooth. "Or, he used to be."

"If he left you, he has shitty judgment," he countered matter-of-factly as he stroked her hair. "Can't be great and have questionable judgment. They're incongruent. That's not presumption. That's fact sweetheart."

The endearment pierced Farrah.

"You don't know him so please don't judge him." She didn't know why, but it was important that he see Aaron through her eyes.

"I don't have to know him. I know plenty of men like him."

"What do you think he – and these plenty of men – are like?" she said, stopping mid-circle in her tracing on his chest.

"Indecisive," he said, lightly tugging on a handful of her hair to make her turn and look up at him. "Men like that … as soon as their toy is taken away and another starts playing with it, they decide they want it back, even though they've moved on to new toys."

"Nice to be thought of as a toy," she said sarcastically, forcing herself not to lose eye contact with him. His blue eyes were a deep well of knowledge; knowledge she wasn't ready to ingest.

"Sorry. Bad analogy, but the point stands. No man leaves a woman the way you said he did you. That's a dick move, pardon the obvious pun. It was cowardice, which says a lot about him. … Why do you even want to go to this wedding?"

"I was invited," she said, as if that explained everything.

"And saying no wasn't an option?" he said, his eyebrows shooting up in surprise.

"Not in my circle. If you're invited, you go. You show support. This is just the way things are in my world. That, and his father and mine and many of the guests are business associates. It wouldn't look good to just blow off the wedding. Besides, I don't want him to think I'm still sore over it."

"Sounds very incestuous, your circle," Finn noted. "And you have a right to be sore – forever if you want. Why are you expected to forgive what he did to you? Crazy if you ask me."

"Perhaps, but also maybe, just maybe, I want to show him what he gave up," she said, dropping her gaze.

Finn studied her. "I'd say your heart is hoping that he doesn't go through with it. My bet is that you're hoping that he takes one look at you and realizes that you've been the one all along."

"That's not true," Farrah denied. "I want revenge."

"Yet again, that beautiful mouth of yours says one thing, while your heart is hoping for another."

"You don't know what you're talking about," Farrah said, hooding her eyes with her lashes.

"I know only too well. Heartache is heartache. And the wishes are the same – to live happily ever after with the one we love," he said wistfully. "This is your wish, and it's ok."

"But that's not my wish. It's not!" Farrah insisted, moving away from him to lean back against the headboard of her bed.

"You can lie to me Farrah, but please don't lie to yourself. Those are the worse lies of all," Finn said. "That being said – and even though I think he's an undeserving bloke – I'll help you get him back, if that is truly your wish."

"You will!" Farrah said, perking up excitedly.

"I will. But under one condition," he said, nestling her back into the pit of his arm.

"And that is?" Farrah asked, peering up at him.

"That you don't cut me off prematurely from this fabulous pussy of yours. Sudden withdrawal could give me blue balls for life," he laughed.

"You're serious? You'll do it? You'll go to the wedding with me?"

"Unlike your bloke, I am a man of my word," he laughed. "I could use a weekend out of the city. As long as we're back by Tuesday, I'm free to accompany you. I will shower you with love and passionate attention. You'll be the envy of every woman there."

"And quite possibly some men too," Farrah giggled as his hand rounded up a pert breast.

Finn frowned at that.

"This is New York," she said, a smile tickling her full lips. "And it is the Hamptons. Farrah laughed as she swatted at his hand. "For the record, it's not just the attention I look forward to you slathering me with," Farrah teased. "You are an extremely handsome man. Why are you single?" she asked as he pushed a piece of her hair out of her eyes with one hand, and pulled her on top of him with the other.

Farrah squealed in delight; the answer to her question the last thing she cared about at the moment.

Chapter 5

""Normally, I do the driving," Finn said, as he admired her gun-silver Jeep Wrangler. He fingered the chrome bumper and noted the chrome step-up as he swung his 6'1" frame into the passenger seat. "Nice. Surprising. But, nice."

"Surprising how?" Farrah asked, as she clicked her seat belt.

She admired the fit of his snug Levi's, and the toned muscle of his arms. Another white t-shirt. She found herself wondering if he had a stack of them, or if he'd done laundry. The thought of him doing the simple domesticated task made her thoughts turn in directions she didn't dare give too much thought. It would be so easy to have him around all the time.

He's a stranger! Farrah admonished herself. A very yummy stranger, but a stranger nonetheless. And all she knew at the moment was that her giddiness at seeing him after three days was insane. She'd missed him. Seeing him again made her feel more alive than she had in years. That thought startled her. How could you be less than alive and not know it? She peered over at him, the electricity between them practically crackling to visibility.

His baby blues caught her doe-like browns as he clicked his seat belt. "You seem more the luxury sports car type: Porsche, Mercedes, BMW," Finn said, loving the way color flooded her cheeks.

Farrah grinned. "Boring, boring and boring. I've actually had two of the three. My first car was a Porsche. Got it for my sixteenth birthday. The second was a Mercedes. That one was a going away to college gift."

"Spoiled little rich girl," Finn said.

"My parents are rich. I'm not," Farrah amended.

"And is that what you aspire to? To be rich?"

Farrah cut her eyes at him.

"Ah, it's to marry rich. I momentarily forgot the purpose of this little trip. Got it," he said.

"You don't get anything about me," Farrah said, annoyed that he would think such a thing about her, especially after the thoughts she was having about him. Then she got annoyed with herself for caring what he thought about her. After Monday, she'd never see him again.

"I'd say there is one thing I get about you. One thing I get very well," Finn said, reaching over to slid his hand between her legs."

Farrah gasped and slapped at his hand. "I'm driving in case you haven't noticed."

"I noticed. I notice everything about you Farrah Jane."

Farrah blushed again and kept her eyes on the road. It was going to be hard not to pull off to the side of the road and pounce on him for a quickie.

She breathed deeply, doing her best to tamp down the heat that was rising in her as she chanced a look over at Finn. He was smiling broadly, the beauty of it making her snatch her gaze back to the road. Dear lord this man was creating havoc with her psyche big time! She spoke up to try to regain some semblance of calm. "You never answered my question."

"What question was that?" Finn asked.

Farrah accelerated as they hit the Long Island Expressway.

"Why are you single? I asked you the other day, remember? You never answered."

"If I remember correctly, it's because we got a little sidetracked," he grinned.

Farrah blushed – yet again. At this rate, she was going to have to buy a new tone of blush to match her always heightened color. "That we did," she grinned back, remembering their last coupling.

Her va-jay-jay was still recovering from the marathon sex they'd had in the approximately fourteen hours they'd spent together that first night and the next morning. Yeah, she'd counted.

He'd been headed out after a leisurely breakfast of coffee, a fruit salad, yogurt and cheese toast. She was still in her bathrobe from the shower she'd eventually taken. Standing in her open doorway, she'd stood on tiptoe to give him a kiss to thank him for agreeing to accompany her to the wedding – and all kinds of hellish passion had broken loose.

***

Her living room wall served as a bed. He'd pushed her up against it, lifted her and slammed his cock home one last time. All without breaking the kiss that had ignited it all.

Farrah orgasmed so hard that her legs, which had been wrapped tightly around his waist, fell limp against him.

Finn grabbed a fistful of her hair and pulled her head to the side. He whispered in her ear, "He was a fool to let you go."

He zipped his jeans, planted a hard kiss on her lips and left her standing there, practically naked as he closed the door softly behind him.
***

Farrah had dropped to her knees and sobbed after Finn left her wilted, satiated body by her front door.

How could a perfect stranger recognize her value, and Aaron, the man she'd given everything to for years, discard her without even so much as a goodbye? God she hated him. Or, was it as Finn said, that she wanted him back.

One of her mother's favorite songs came to mind; *It's a Thin Line between Love and Hate*. She had been the sweetest woman in the world, and Aaron had turned her into the meanest woman in the world – someone she hadn't recognized since he'd walked out on her. And this weekend, she was going to get her revenge.

And then what? a little voice had said.
***

"Penny for your thoughts," Finn said, wondering where she'd disappeared to for the last few minutes.

Intuitively, Farrah hit her blinker to signal a lane change. "Are you going to answer my question?" she responded, looking over at him.

"As soon as I'm sure you're fully present enough to hear my answer. Where were you just now?" he asked.

"The interrogation of me is over. It's time for me to interrogate you, and the question on the table is, 'Why are you single?'"

"Why is anyone single?" he countered. "I haven't met the right person, not ready to settle down, busy with my career; all of the above."

"What do you do?" Farrah asked, a bit embarrassed that she didn't know. He'd been in the most intimate parts of her, but outside of his name and that he was very obviously from Ireland, she knew very little about him except that he made a mean cup of coffee and was excellent at scrounging up an impromptu meal.

She'd meant to get the total run down before he left that morning, but before too many questions could be asked and answered about him, they'd somehow managed to mostly talk about her and her relationship with Aaron. Looking back, she wondered if he'd done that on purpose. And if so, why?

Priscilla's words rang in her head again: *you've become little more than a ... well a common, loose woman. You need to get control of yourself; get control of your life.* Maybe she was right. As attracted as she was to him and as normal as he seemed, he was still a complete stranger who could be anyone from a wanted felon to psychopath. Who was he? The urgency to know rushed over her.

"I'm a painter," he said suddenly, breaking Farrah's thoughts.

"Really?" Farrah said in surprise. That was practically the last thing she would have guessed. Model; maybe even new age spiritual guru, considering how laid back he was. But artist. Her mind never would have gone there.

She looked over at him, furrowing one brow.

He was nonplussed. Stares made most people uncomfortable, especially when they didn't really know a person. Not Finn. He ingested her stare; his gaze inviting her to drink her fill of him. And that more than anything, revealed his artist soul.

Farrah had known a few artists in her day, and they seemed to have a deeper connection to the truth than most mere mortals.

"You seem surprised," he noted.

"I am," Farrah admitted.

"Why?"

"Are you deliberately trying not to answer my questions? I feel like you're evading; like you don't want me to get to know you."

"Perhaps a reflex action," he said. In fact, there's nothing he'd like more than to invite Farrah Jane into his world.

Now it was Farrah's turn to remain quiet.

The wind sailing through the windows whirled the electricity between them around. It landed on Finn, prompting him to explain his life's work in away that he'd only shared with two other people – his mother, and his last lover. Perhaps he'd moved to quickly in breaking things off.

"I'm a painter because I simply can't *not* be. It runs through my veins like blood; my chest like air; my being like survival. It's the only thing I know how to be."

"Mercy," Farrah said, letting out a low whistle. "That's straight-up poetry."

Finn felt naked, exposed. But not vulnerable. It was like being Michelangelo's *David;* he stood proud in his bareness.

"How did you develop that kind of passion?"

"I didn't," he said, pausing, searching for the right words to explain. "In my opinion, you don't develop passion. You simply lean into it when you realize it's there. Art is the one thing that taught me to stand in my truth. It made me realize that if you stand in your truth, there is very little to hide from or be afraid of. Once I stopped running away from that reality, life got easier because I knew it would be my life's work."

His explanation only deepened her insane attraction to him. And now that his vocation had been revealed, she could totally see it. He was definitely passionate. There was an intenseness about him. He also seemed to see things clearly, a trait she envied. *He's a fool to let you go. You want him back.* The observation stabbed at her subconscious. *Could he be right?*

"Thank you for sharing that with me. You could have stopped at, 'I'm a painter.'"

Finn nodded his head and chuckled. The fact that she realized he'd revealed a deep truth made him desire her even more. There was a wavelength their subconscious was communicating on that vibrated the conscious mind. He wondered if that was the pull he felt to her.

"What do you paint? Are you genre specific? What medium do you specialize in: oils, acrylics--"

"So you know about art?"

"You can't be a spoiled, little rich girl raised in New York City and not have a solid foundation of the arts. It would be … uncivilized," she said, clutching imaginary pearls.

He laughed out loud, and Farrah found herself thinking that she'd say almost anything to hear that sound over and over again. "Don't keep a girl in suspense, Mr. O'Hare. Tell me about your painting."

"I actually specialize in a technique known as encaustic."

"Encaustic? Encaustic," Farrah repeated. "I'm stumped. I don't know what that is."

"Don't feel bad. Many don't. It's a very old painting technique, dating back to the ancient Egyptians."

"Now you've really piqued my interest. What makes it so obscure?" Farrah asked, still racking her brain for something on the artistic medium, but coming up empty.

"It's not an easy technique to master. In fact, I'm not sure you ever fully master it; you learn enough to make you appreciate the beauty of it – and frustrate your soul enough to want to continue," he said, unconsciously moving his fingers as if a paint brush was in it. The movement made Farrah smile.

"That's very poetic," Farrah said. "Do you write poetry as well? Most artists I know can't seem to contain themselves to one thing."

Finn gave a slight smile, and continued. "That's because creativity is rarely one dimensional. It's like love. You can express it in many different ways."

"Yet more poetry," Farrah said softly, somewhat hypnotized by the simple, but profoundly deep, observation.

Finn's voice became more melodic, his Irish lilt even more pronounced as he explained his form of painting to her. It was as if he was speaking about an old, highly missed lover. "To answer your question, what makes encaustic painting so obscure is that it involves working in different mediums."

"At Farrah's quizzical look, he continued. "You have to add pigment to hot beeswax, then add that to wood – a piece of specially prepared wood. Then, you have to sculpt the liquid before it cools. That's what makes it kind of difficult to master. You know how quickly wax cools."

"I can imagine the skill required," Farrah said. "What drew you to such an obscure technique?"

"I kind of fell into it. I stayed with it because it creates complex works full of dimension and color. I haven't found another painting medium where I can achieve the kind of depth I like to have in my pieces."

"You said you fell into it."

Finn nodded.

"How?"

"I grew up in a little fishing village on the northern coast of Ireland called Emmy Isles; short for Emerald Island. We lived closed to the water and I used to collect driftwood as a kid to amuse myself. There happened to be plenty of candles around, as my mum loved them. And my father was a house painter, so there was always plenty of paint around too. It wasn't artistic paint, of course, but it was paint. I have always liked creating things – especially with my hands. My mind ... if I'm not creating, if my hands aren't busy, I can't function."

"You definitely have a set of skilled hands," Farrah noted naughtily, remembering the way his fingers had slid in and out of her. She shifted slightly in her seat.

If she wasn't mistaken, it was his turn to blush. It softened his features, making him look younger. "It helps when you have a subject that was made for exploration. And you, woman, you were made for a man's touch," he said, reaching over and running a hand over her right breast. Instead of objecting, as he expected her to, she leaned into the caress.

The feel of his hands on her body was as natural as breathing; like that's where they were supposed to be. Farrah glanced at him, a smile curving her lips. Her eyes turned back to the road. "With your passion, I bet you're highly successful."

"You'd lose that bet," Finn responded. It was the first time she'd seen a hint of disappointment in him.

"Why?" she asked.

"Being an artist doesn't pay the bills. At least not an unknown artist."

"Money isn't everything," Farrah said.

"Only someone who's always had plenty of it can say something like that," Finn noted, without animosity or jealousy. It was a plain life observation.

"So where can I see your work?"

"I'll let you know on Tuesday," he grinned, the lightness back in his being.

"What's happening on Tuesday? And who says we'll be seeing each other after Monday?"

"Hmmm, true. That does present a problem, especially as my job is to help you win your fiance--"

"Ex-fiance," Farrah interjected. "And stop saying that," she snapped.

"Saying what?" Finn countered. "That you want your fiance back? You do. Remember when I told you that once I accepted my destiny, life got easier?"

Farrah's eyes remained glued to the road. Her lips were a thin line *of 'I don't want to hear what you're going to say.'* "What's that got to do with the price of tea in China?"

"Why is it so hard for you to admit that you still love this man; that you want him back? There's no shame in that. In fact, there's power in it. If you unlock your heart to him, he just may unlock his to you." The words left a bitter taste in his mouth. He licked his lips.

"He's getting married. Or have you forgotten that we're on the way to his w-e-d-d-i-n-g," Farrah spelled out."

"And w-e-d-d-i-n-g-s are canceled all the time, especially if a soulmate is waiting in the wings." *I don't even know this dude, and I know he's not her soulmate, his subconscious said.* Finn shook his head to clear it. *Stay on mission,* he admonished himself.

"He made his position clear when he left me," Farrah said, her lips a thin, pinkish line.

"Yet here you are. On your way to his wedding. Jumping through hoops in hopes of getting him back. Disguising it as revenge. What if ... just what if Farrah, he was terrified that you would reject him? That his pride would not let him come back to you? And he runs off to marry the first chit that comes along because he knows he's lost the only woman he'll ever love?"

"Why are you doing this? Saying these things?" she said. That was only one of the scenarios she'd imagined these last few months. And now, here he, a total stranger was, pumping hope into her imaginings. That made it more real. More attainable. And it made her a damn fool! No, she wanted revenge alright, and she was going to have it.

"I say it because destiny is real. And you only get one life to live. Why would you so easily give up the man you love? If you love him, fight for him if you think he's worth it."

"Do you think that could be a possibility?" Farrah asked. "What you said – do men think like that?"

"I'm going to tell you a little secret about men ... most of us are cowards when it comes to women; especially women we love. That's why we'd literally break every bone in our body to avoid falling in love. When you add that to the fact that we hate to admit that we're wrong, it's a recipe for disaster."

"So you think Aaron is afraid to admit that he made a mistake with me?"

"It's human nature not to admit mistakes. And men are harder-wired not to admit them than women are."

"That doesn't answer my question," Farrah said. "Do you think Aaron thinks that?"

Finn paused and looked at her discreetly from under his sombrero of lashes. Such hope, such fragility on such a beautiful face. He knew he'd be re-creating that look in his work at some point. It would haunt him if he didn't. He measured his words out in small scoops of hope for her.

"I don't know because I don't know him. For all of the generalities I just spewed, every man is different. You're obviously still in love with him. There has to be something unique about him that's keeping that love alive, otherwise you wouldn't be going through all this. I personally can't wait to meet the chap who's making a woman like you behave like this."

Farrah felt like he could see right through her. And while she hated it, she felt relieved at the same time. There'd been no one she could unload on about her true feelings for Aaron. She was too embarrassed to admit them to her friends and family. A complete stranger was the perfect answer.

"You're right," Farrah admitted. "I do still love him." It felt damn good to get it out, to say it freely without feeling like a fool. Finn was a stranger; there were no ties now or in the future. Ever since he'd left her, she'd been angry and hurt; hiding the truth from herself. It had drained her emotionally. Damn near driven her to a breakdown.

Finn looked over at her. He hated to hear her admit it, but he admired her courage in doing so.

Farrah continued. "But I also hate him for what he did to me. He didn't have to leave me like that. That's the part that hurt the most."

"So one part of you wants him to feel the kind of pain he caused you, and the other part wants him back. It's a war within and you haven't quite figured out how it's all going to play out this weekend."

"Exactly! How did you know?"

"As I've said before, some feelings are universal Farrah. And I do know a little piece of you; a very intimate piece of you."

"As you said, that's just sex."

"I lied, a little," he said sheepishly. "What we had was sex. But it wasn't *just* sex. What passed between us was something more."

Farrah felt the same, but dismissed it. She was in love with someone else, and although she did feel a crazy draw to this stranger, she'd filed that under endorphins released by good sex. She was surprised to hear his take.

"Life. It gives you little surprises from time to time."

"True. And it also demands answers."

"What do you mean?" Farrah asked.

"Your current conundrum. You do realize that sooner or later, you're going to have to ask yourself what it is that you really want as it relates to your ex? Not what is expected of you by someone or something else. But, what is it that Farrah wants."

"I suppose subconsciously, I did know that," Farrah said slowly.

"The time to decide will reveal itself," Finn said as her forehead crinkled.

"I'm hope you're right. ... So tell me this, do you think if we'd met under different circumstances – never mind," Farrah said, cutting herself short. How could she even think of being with another when it was Aaron her heart desired.

It's just, Finn seemed to understand her on more than a surface level. She'd never had that from anyone in her life. Ever. It felt like home, for lack of a better word. She wondered what it would be like to have that kind of intrinsic understanding all the time. The thought brightened and saddened her at the same time.

"So tell me more about you Mr. Finneas O'Hare," Farrah teased, needing to lighten the mood. "How long have you been in the U.S.? How long do you plan to stay?"

Chapter 6

"We're here," Farrah said, her fingers tightening around the steering wheel as they drove up a long, circular driveway to a huge mansion with dark-gray, shaker siding.

"Shouldn't you be getting ready to release the steering wheel?" Finn said, noting the choke hold she had on it.

"You're supposed to be relaxing me," Farrah said as her Jeep idled. There were at least half a dozen vehicles in front of them. Range Rovers. Mercedes. Jaguars; all luxury.

Finn noticed several valets waiting to park the expensive cars, and attendants waiting to help guests unload their luggage.

"Remember our deal," Farrah said.

"To the letter," Finn said, smiling. "We are madly in love. We met at a charity networking event where I had donated one of my paintings. And you, on behalf of your company, were the high bidder. It was practically love at first sight, and we haven't left each other's side since."

"Great," Farrah said. "Oh, a couple of more things right quick. Did I ask you how old you were? I forget. And where do you live?"

"I'm 32, and I live in my van," Finn said, as a valet pulled open Farrah's door and a screaming woman ran up to her.

Chapter 7

"You made it! You made it! You made it!" Brynwen said, jumping up and down.

"I did, I did, I did," Farrah laughed, hugging the still-screaming woman, as she looked over at Finn, who'd exited the Jeep.

Did he just say he lived in his van?!

"I'm so happy you're here. You have no idea!"

"And what, pray tell, is this over-the-top exuberance all about? Married life in the suburbs hasn't changed you a bit. You're still the screechiest, sweetest woman I know," Farrah laughed, hugging her overly excited friend again.

"I'm pregnant," Brynwen announced breathlessly, unable to hold her good news in a second longer.

"You're ... you're going to have a baby?" Farrah said in awe.

Brynwen shook her head, unable to speak. Tears formed in her enormous brown eyes. "I've never been so happy and so scared in my whole life. I still don't quite believe it," she said, one hand splayed across her ever-so-slight bump.

If you didn't know her, you'd never know Brynwen was pregnant. A yoga devotee since their freshman year of college, Farrah could tell. Brynwen had the tightest, flattest abs she'd ever seen on anyone. The slight bump she sported, which would pass for the flattest of flat abs on anyone else, was a sure sign that she was indeed with child.

Of the half-dozen or so young women in her group from grade school to college, everyone agreed that Brynwen was made to be a mother. But she and her husband had struggled to get pregnant since they got married just over two years ago.

"Oh sweetie, I'm so happy for you. Don't be scared. Rejoice! Whatever comes, you got this. You so go this," Farrah reassured her friend, tears moistening her eyes too.

Her tears were for her friend, but they were also for a dream she'd given up long ago. Just getting Aaron to give her an engagement ring had taken seven years. She'd told herself that if he never married her, just being with him was enough. But seeing Brynwen's joy at being pregnant kicked her uterus into gear. She knew without a doubt that in the end, it never would have been enough. She wanted children; had always wanted them. It was yet another dream she'd been willing to sacrifice for his love. The intensity of the realization shook her.

What do I really want from this weekend? she asked herself for the zillionth time this week. The question had settled in her mind like a shroud; the mist of it hiding the answer from her heart.

"You think so Farrah? You think everything will be okay?" Brynwen asked, her eyes so full of fear that Farrah hugged her again. "Of course sweetie. You're young. You're strong. You're fit. Sometimes mother nature needs a jump-start, which you obviously got. But you can take it from there. And you will. You will have a beautiful little red-headed terror for me to spoil senseless in what – six, seven months?"

"I'm actually almost five months along. So just over four months," Brynwen revealed.

"You look like you're barely beginning," Farrah said. "And you're way past your first trimester, so that's great."

"I know, and the doctor said everything looks good. But I'm still so nervous," Brynwen admitted, holding her middle protectively.

"Bryn being past the first trimester is huge. I know you know this. Worrying won't change anything. And stressing could be detrimental to you and the baby. Stress is real sweetie. So try to relax and enjoy this pregnancy. It's your first one and you're missing out on the joy of the miracle you're carrying," Farrah said, holding her friend's hand tight.

"You always did know what to say to make me feel better. You're right. I can't control what's going to happen. My doctor said pretty much the same thing. I think I just needed to hear it from someone other than her to make it real."

"Your doctor wouldn't lie to you honey," Farrah said.

"I know, but she's paid to worry. And I naturally worry. But hearing it come from someone who cares for me, but is not afraid to tell me what I *don't* want to hear; it just hit home better. You've always been a straight shooter. Just one of the things I love about you," Brynwen said as she pulled Farrah into a bear hug.

Farrah noticed a pair of piercing blue eyes staring at her; a dare in them. He was daring her to confront the truth about what she wanted from this weekend. She knew beyond a shadow of a doubt that that's what that stare was all about.

Farrah felt like a fraud. Damn him and those all-knowing baby blues!

"Then that makes the trip alone worth it," Farrah said, pulling back from her friend.

"After what Priscilla said, I didn't think you were coming," Brynwen said.

"What did Priscilla say?" Farrah asked as nonchalantly as possible, crossing her arms over her chest. She didn't realize that her body language betrayed her coolness.

But Finn did. God she wished he'd stop looking at her like that; like she was some kind of fraud.

"Priscilla said she thought you'd chicken out because you're still in love with Aar--"

"Brynwen, this is Finn," Farrah said, practically pushing her friend into Finn in her haste to cut her off. "He's ... we're--"

"I'm Farrah's other half," Finn said, barely containing his amusement at the situation. "Nice to meet you Brynwen. Farrah's told me about her girl posse, as she termed it. Nice to finally put a face to a name, and congrats on the baby."

"Oh Farrah, he's divine," Brynwen giggled upon hearing Finn's Irish accent.

Farrah almost laughed out loud. Brynwen had always been a sucker for an accent.

"He is indeed," Farrah said, thinking her friend had no idea just how heavenly he was. The blush that crept up her cheeks did not have to be faked.

Upon Brynwen's giddiness at being in the presence of Finn, Farrah recalled a summer trip they'd taken between their junior and senior years of high school with their respective parents. They'd all vacationed in the Caribbean that year – Jamaica. She swore Brynwen spent that entire summer in a constant state of heat, letting herself be caught by more than one smooth-talking Jamaican lad. Their parents would have padlocked them in their rooms if they knew even a quarter of the shenanigans they pulled on that trip.

Brynwen wasted no time beginning her Q&A with the handsome Irishman. "So Finn," she said, looping her arm through his. "Tell me, what is it that you do?"

Finn patted her arm lightly, and looked over his shoulder at Farrah.

Farrah smiled and turned to retrieve her make-up case from the back seat of her Jeep. An attendant grabbed the luggage.

"Follow me miss," the young man said.

Farrah nodded her head and fell into step slightly behind him. When she turned around again, Finn and Brynwen were nowhere in sight. She smiled to herself. If she knew Brynwen, Finn was being introduced to a circle of curious young women: half of them single and hot for him; a couple of them married and hot for him, and the others prudish enough not to admit that they're hot for him. But flush they'd all be; that she would be ton.

She'd seen Finn when he unintentionally turned on the charm. Intentional charm, and he could make any woman in his vicinity drown in her own juices. She knew, because she'd been the recipient of his intentional charms.

Farrah felt flushed.

"Farrah," a soul-crushingly familiar voice said.

Farrah's head snapped up, and her gaze got lost in the obsidian eyes of the man her heart had beat for, for almost a decade.

"Aaron," she said, her breath barely escaping her throat.

Chapter 8

"Still carrying around a suitcase full of warpaint, I see," Aaron said, noting her makeup case. "Not that you need it," he added.

He always had to get in a jab first, Farrah's mind registered. That had been one thing she'd never liked about him But his passive-aggressive nature was nothing compared to the sweet side of him; the side that had made her fall in love with him all those years ago.

"Something I tell her all the time," Finn said, taking the case from Farrah's hand. "Any man with eyes can see that," he said, his blue eyes firmly on Farrah, letting her know that he knew exactly who Aaron was.

"Aaron Montblanc LeGrew," Aaron said. "I don't think we've had the pleasure," he said, his eyes conveying anything but wanting to make pleasantries.

"Finn," Finn replied. Aaron's name sounded ostentatious compared to Finn's simple introduction. It was almost like he did it on purpose, to underscore how pompous he thought Aaron was.

"Finneas O'Hare," Farrah filled in.

"The boyfriend," Aaron declared rather than asked, noting his tight grip on Farrah's waist. His eyes seemed glued to where Finn touched her, as if to ward him off.

Finn tightened his grip. "Where I come from, only lads say boyfriend," he said, pulling a devilish smile out of his back pocket. "Men don't refer to each other as boys."

Farrah noted a slight pool of color in Aaron's alabaster cheeks.

"So what exactly would you say you are to Farrah then, Mr. O'Hare?"

"It's--" Farrah started.

"Man, mate, partner," he said, looking at Farrah. "Take your pick."

"Farrah?" Aaron said. "Your title?"

"This is the twenty-first century. Are titles still necessary?" Farrah evaded, with a small smile.

"I disagree," Aaron responded. "Titles tell us where we stand," Aaron said.

"In that case, I'd say lover. Puts a neat little bow on everything," Finn responded, looking deeply into Farrah's eyes. "Any other questions?"

Aaron looked at Farrah. He could tell she was unnerved by the exchange.

"What part of fair Ireland are you from?" Aaron asked, needing to know more about this stranger. His gaze was still glued to Farrah, savoring seeing her face again. He'd missed her more than he realized.

"Finneas O'Hare in the flesh. Wonders never cease," a husky female voice said." The slits of her cat-green gaze sliced through the arm firmly around Farrah's waist.

What the hell was Farrah doing with her lover?! Priscilla thought.

Chapter 9

Farrah could swear Finn went pale at his name on Priscilla's lips. But like a chameleon lizard that changed color to suit its surroundings, the flash of pale was gone as quickly as it had appeared.

"Priscilla," Finn returned smoothly, training his laser-blue gaze on Farrah's friend. Or, ex-friend as the case may be.

Farrah's eyes widened. "You know each other?" she asked, feeling stupid for asking such an obvious question. She squirmed in Finn's grasp.

Finn inclined his head slightly, looking at Priscilla as he tightened his grip on Farrah to still her. He noted the large, pear-cut diamond on the ring finger of Priscilla's left hand. *That was new.*

"From the gallery," Priscilla hastily explained. "I introduced Finn to his agent, who obviously wasted no time getting to work. Congrats on the upcoming show. I'm not surprised."

"Show?" Farrah parroted.

"You didn't tell me your new little fling was with an about-to-be-famous artist," Priscilla said, eyeing Farrah. "Half the people here know his work, if not the face. But everyone will know all of him soon."

"I don't understand," Farrah said, totally confused. She felt like she was the only one who didn't know what the hell was going on! This was not working out like she planned. At all.

"I was going to surprise you once things were set in stone, sweetheart," Finn said, his gaze telling her to keep her cool; that he had things under control. "Obviously, Priscilla has the inside track," Finn said, his gaze flitting back to Priscilla as he held possessively onto Farrah.

"Perhaps you've been too busy, ah, getting it in – shall we say – to pick up the latest issue of *hAuRTe Couture*," Priscilla said to Farrah, referencing the go-to Hamptons art magazine. A smile was pinned on her perfectly painted lips, disguising her tawdry comment as a 'new couple' joke for the crowd around them. But Farrah knew different. She colored at Priscilla's crudeness.

The smile Priscilla glued on landed nowhere near her frosty green eyes. She continued with her introduction of Finn to the group. "Finneas O'Hare. Remember the name ladies and gentlemen. He is apparently the latest and greatest painter to come along since Picasso. He has a showing coming up next month at the *La Vive* gallery in Soho. The moneyed glitterati are expected to turn out in droves. And apparently, he is not single, which all the ladies will be disappointed to know, I'm sure," she finished.

Farrah wanted to slap her as she stood there giving a rundown on *her Finn* to their friends. Right before her eyes, the spotlight of having rebounded from her ex-fiance to a handsome, talented, about-to-be-famous artist was being stolen by none other than Priscilla – a woman she could barely stomach these days.

A show. Famous artist. Greatest since Picasso. She needed answers. And Priscilla was apparently the one to give them to her.

Two could play the pasted-on-smile game Farrah decided. "Thanks for the introduction. I couldn't have said it better myself," Farrah said, sliding out of Finn's grasp and grabbing Priscilla by the arm. She threw up an *'Excuse us'* wave as she marched Priscilla out of the group.

The small circle of curious minds that had surrounded them closed in on Finn as soon as she and Priscilla cleared the group.

Farrah noted that Aaron looked on in confusion. *And anger?*

Finn's face, in contrast, was a perfect mask of handsome humor.

What did Aaron have to be angry about, Farrah thought. But her heart jumped. At least it was at least some kind of emotion. She vowed to get to exactly what kind at some point this weekend.

"What the hell was that all about?" Farrah demanded as she slammed the door of the bathroom she'd practically dragged Priscilla through.

Chapter 10

Finn looked at his watch in between the barrage of questions he received from the group around him.

Yes, I miss Ireland.

Practically all my life. Being painter is the only thing I've ever wanted to do.

Never married. No children.

Yes, I hope to some day. Meeting the right woman is key, of course.

"Could that right woman be Farrah? You all would have beautiful babies," Brynwen said.

Finn smiled. "It seems I have quite lucked out," Finn answered evasively.

"You've got baby fever," Erica, one of Farrah and Brynwen's friends, said. "Ever since we were in kindergarten, all you've ever wanted to do his have babies. I don't think Farrah's in that club."

"Farrah is married to her career," Aaron said.

"Maybe I do have baby fever," Brynwen said, "but I think Farrah would make a great mother. Dreams can change," she said in defense of her friend.

"That they can," Finn said.

"See," Brynwen said, almost triumphantly. "Who better to know than her lover?" she said, grinning warmly at Finn.

"Some things are absolutes," Aaron insisted. "And one thing I know about Farrah is that she's always been married to her career."

"The right mate can change many things," Finn said, looking pointedly at Aaron. "Take your impending nuptials. From what I hear, you weren't very keen on marriage. But obviously, that changed when you met the right one."

A hush fell over the group.

Twin peaks of color flooded Aaron's cheeks. He felt heat running up his neck.

Brynwen could barely contain her laughter. She wondered if Farrah had told her exactly why Aaron was marrying Adelaide. She couldn't contain herself. "Finn makes a good point, don't you think Aaron? All it takes is to meet the right person to change everything."

Aaron swallowed. He'd never liked Brynwen. She was a goody two shoes with an all-knowing attitude he found claustrophobic. "You have a point; the key being, meeting the right person," he said, looking from Brynwen to Finn.

"Some of us have to kiss a lot of toads to find the one. Seems like Farrah's toad-kissing days are over," Brynwen fired back.

"One woman's toad is another woman's Prince," a voice from just outside the group said.

Several nervous pairs of eyes landed on the woman as she joined the group and slid her hand onto Aaron's forearm.

"Adelaide," Erica said.

Brynwen spoke up. "I couldn't have said it better myself," she giggled, as Aaron's fiance eyed the group.

"I don't think we've had the pleasure," Adelaide said, directing her attention to Finn. She already knew everyone else in the group.

***

"So you're the cause of the excited buzz around here," Adelaide said. She and Finn had broken away from the group, and were engrossed in conversation in a small table by a big window in the receiving room of the mansion.

"I think that's a little overstating it. What everybody is excited about is the wedding of the decade," Finn responded.

"Don't try to change the subject Mr. O'Hare. Tell me about your work. I can't remember the last time I've heard such excitement about an artist."

Finn found himself engrossed in conversation with Adelaide. She was not only very knowledgeable about art, but a great patron of it too. He'd told her about several pieces that would premier in his show, and she'd committed to purchasing one sight unseen.

"I'm flattered, but I can't let you do that," he said.

"And just how do you propose to stop me?" Adelaide said, cheerfully, but firmly.

This was a woman who always got her way, Finn thought. Poor Aaron didn't stand a chance if he thought he could play games with her, even though it was evident she was stupidly, truly in love with him.

"Very well. But to appease my artist soul, come to the show. You might see something you like better."

"I highly doubt it," Adelaide said.

"You're very decisive. A rare quality," Finn said, liking the young woman. She was nowhere near beautiful, but her intelligence pushed her into the attractive category for him. He loved a beautiful woman as much as the next bloke, but it was intelligence that kept his interest.

"And you're very perceptive, Mr. O'Hare. A rare gift," Adelaide returned.

They locked eyes for a second – a mutual respect passing between them.

"Now, I'm even more glad that Farrah came this weekend."

"May I ask why?" Finn said, curious. In the short time he'd spent with her, he knew that Adelaide never said anything without a purpose.

"Let's just say it's time for all games to cease. Shall we rejoin the group? I fear my poor fiance is going to bore a hole through you if he looks over here any harder," she said smiling.

"No man likes to see his woman with another," Finn teased.

"Illusions. It's nice to let yourself live under them from time to time." Finn noted the tinge of sadness lacing Adelaide's words. They stood and went to rejoin the group they'd left standing a little while ago.

Apparently, she and Finn had become the talk of the room. The bride-to-be in deep conversation with the groom-to-be's ex-fiance's boyfriend. Adelaide chuckled as she looked at Finn.

"Private joke?" he asked.

"A little excitement before the big day," Adelaide said mischievously. "You have to give the society pages something to talk about besides which designer the bride wore."

"Your husband-to-be is in for quite a ride through life," Finn smiled just before they got within earshot of the curious group that had been watching them.

"He has no idea," Adelaide said, laughing out loud.

Chapter 11

“What the hell did you tell Bryn,” Farrah hissed. “I assumed you had enough common sense to keep your damn mouth shut about what I told you about me and Finn.”

“I wasn’t aware that I was supposed to keep your little fuckboy a secret,” Priscilla said, still rubbing the arm she’d yanked away from Farrah. “This had better not bruise. My dress is strapless,” she said, surveying the spot.

“You’re going to have bigger issues to worry about than a bruise on your arm if you say one more word about how I met Finn,” Farrah warned, a finger squarely pointed in Priscilla’s face. “I’m not playing with you.”

“What are you going to do? Beat me up? Really Farrah, you are descending into ghetto-hood.”

Farrah’s hand moved without her permission. It had to, otherwise, how could she account for the red welt across her friend’s face?

Priscilla yelped like the little ugly rat dog she carried around everywhere. “You … you hit me,” she said, holding her left cheek with both hands. “You hit me,” she repeated, a storm brewing in her feline-green eyes.

Farrah was well aware of that look. She’d been on the receiving end of it many times – from grade school all the way through college. In an instant, she swore it would be the last time. The word ghetto-hood was the last straw.

“I’ve put up with your snide remarks, your outright bullying and being your token *I’m not racist’* black friend for years. This is where it stops,” Farrah said. “Don’t you ever speak to me like that again. Ever,” Farrah warned.

“Or what?” Priscilla spat. “If it wasn’t for me, you wouldn’t have had any friends. And I’ve never treated you or thought of you like a token friend,” she said.

For a second, her statement rattled Farrah because her ex-friend almost seemed sincere. But then, Priscilla was good at faking things. It was one of her gifts, as Farrah knew all too well.

"You have," Farrah insisted. "Or does treating others like second-class citizens come so naturally that you don't realize when you're doing it?"

"I--" Priscilla started.

"That was a rhetorical question," Farrah said, putting her hand up as she cut the other woman off. "I don't care which it is. All I know is this: I will no longer be talked about, or down to, by you. And that includes sharing what I've told you as a supposed friend. You will keep your damn mouth shut about me and any aspect of my life, or that slap is just an appetizer of what will be coming your way."

"Are you threatening me?" Priscilla asked.

"No, I'm giving you an ass-whooping promise. Don't fuck with me Priscilla. You won't like the consequences," Farrah said.

"I think you forget who you're dealing with Farrah. We are no longer school girls. We're grown women, with grown women weapons at our disposal."

"Are *you* threatening *me*?" Farrah said, almost relishing the prospect. She didn't realize until that moment just how sick and tired she was of the way Priscilla had treated her all these years.

If she expressed interest in a boy, the next week, he was Priscilla's play thing.

If she expressed interest in running for student body president, all of a sudden, Priscilla had a full-fledged campaign under way.

If she decided to pledge a sorority, Priscilla was all of a sudden interested.

And Farrah had accepted it; her parents insisting that it was simple good-natured competition and she was lucky to have a friend who pushed her to be better.

Now though, she wondered, what was at the root of it? She didn't have the energy or desire to care. Being back in the confines of her circle of life-long friends was drowning her in memories she'd rather forget. Priscilla's next words snatched her back to the present.

"You want your little fuck boy's career to die before it even gets started? You want to keep that job you're so crazy about? You want your name to be synonymous with whore wherever you go? Choose your poison sweetheart, because if you fuck with me, poison is what you're going to be drinking," Priscilla said, nose to nose with Farrah.

"So it's like that, huh?" Farrah said, a joker-like laugh bubbling from her chest.

Priscilla looked at her like she was a little bit crazy, and a lot out of her ever-lasting mind.

"I've been wondering just how far your hatred of me went. Now I know," Farrah said.

"Why would I hate you? I have everything you've ever wanted. It's you who has always envied me," Priscilla countered.

"You're right. I was jealous of you. But not for the reasons you're thinking. I was jealous that you never had to worry about fitting in. You just did."

A confused expression crossed Priscilla's face.

"But you wouldn't understand that, would you? Of course not," Farrah answered for her. "So let me just say this: cross me, and the games will begin in earnest."

"There's no game you can play that I can't play better," Priscilla vowed. "I invented the rules for the type of game you're just thinking about starting to play," she added emphatically.

"You think so, huh?" Farrah said. "Then like I said, dear friend, let the games begin," Farrah repeated. "For Act 1, I'll start with a little video of you bragging about how you could always fuck the pool boy when your limp-dicked husband couldn't get it up."

Priscilla's mouth formed a shocked 'O'.

Farrah pressed on. "I didn't even know I still had that footage. But lo and beyond, it survived four moves, two boyfriends and three promotions – in a job I do happen to love by the way. How ironic is that?" Farrah laughed.

The truth was, Farrah had only run across the footage because she'd been going through some old photos on her computer of her and Aaron. That's when she'd come across a few videos from Priscilla's bachelorette party – video that their girl posse had declared would never see the light of day. Why she hadn't deleted it when she ran across it a couple of weeks ago, she didn't know. It was almost like her subconscious was at work; knowing that she might one day need it.

She had spent two hours on her bedroom floor, laptop in hand, dry heaving after crying so long and so hard. Her goal was to cry out all the tears from Aaron's final heartbreak before she attended is wedding. That way, there'd be nothing left on the day of. And cry she had – at practically every photo and video clip she clicked on. There were hundreds and hundreds, if not a few thousand, of them. She, Aaron, their friends. Their life in picture and video. And as one of Farrah and Aaron's best friends, Priscilla's face was a constant. She hadn't realized just how close they had all been until she'd spent those hours going through the last decade or so of her life.

Priscilla was the common link between them. She'd known Aaron all her life. Their fathers were close business associates.

Dateless one holiday season, Priscilla had accompanied Farrah to her company's Christmas party. She'd pointed out Aaron as the guy she had a secret crush on. Priscilla had waltzed over, grabbed Aaron by the hand, and presented him to Farrah on a silver platter.

Chapter 12

Almost 10 years ago

"Aaron, Farrah. Farrah, Aaron. I'm going to mingle and let nature take its course," she said, her blonde hair almost brushing her backside as she flounced away from them.

Farrah stood flabbergasted, glued to the spot. When Farrah had asked Priscilla how she could know such a gorgeous man and not want to hump his bones, Priscilla replied, "Who says I haven't?" and winked at Farrah.

"Have you--"

Priscilla cut her off. "Really Farrah. I just served him up like prime rib for you. What more do you want?"

"I know. I'm sorry. Silly question. It's just, he's so gorgeous."

Priscilla smiled. "I guess."

Farrah asked Aaron why he and Priscilla had never dated.

He'd colored, as if he was embarrassed by the question.

Farrah rushed to explain. "It's just, you all have so much in common."

"Maybe that's it; too much in common. You need some kind of friction to create chemistry," Aaron said.

"I see," Farrah said.

"I hope you see more than that. I'm beginning to think the reason is more cosmic," Aaron said, grabbing her hand.

"Cosmic?" Farrah asked, too shy to look him directly in the eye.

"I think the reason it never worked out with Priscilla or anyone else is because I was supposed to meet you."

At that, Farrah looked up at him, not giving another thought to Aaron and Priscilla. Her only thoughts were of her and Aaron – and a future that held all kind of promises.

Chapter 13

Present Day

Nothing had turned out like she wanted, of course. She'd had to practically have a nervous breakdown before he gave her an engagement ring. Then he meets the little chit – the way Farrah referred to his soon-to-be wife – and was engaged to be married after only five months of dating. And obedient little woman that she was, she was following protocol; showing up to wish him happiness, while her heart still swam in a sea of sadness from their breakup.

Protocol. Every damn thing in her world had always been dictated by protocol! But without it, she wasn't sure she knew how to make a decision.

What do you want? Finn had told her she'd eventually have to answer that question. Not based on what her parents wanted. Not based on what her friends thought. Not based on what her ex wanted. But she, Farrah? What did Farrah want?

Revenge? Or a future with Aaron?

Being back among those who'd known her all of her life, the answer should have been clear. Yet, she'd never been more confused.

***

"You're lying," Priscilla said, snapping Farrah back to the present. "If there was video of me saying something like that, you would have told me about it a long time ago. You're just saying that so I'll keep your little pretend boyfriend a secret."

Farrah had never blackmailed a soul in her life, but so help her god, if Priscilla spilled the secret of how she and Finn met, she would release the drunken video of her and her pool-boy dreams for the world to see.

"Try me," Farrah declared. "And not only will I show it to your husband, I'll have a viewing party and broadcast it to everybody."

Priscilla hissed in surprise, her breath sizzling like cold water on hot concrete.

Farrah took triumph in the expression. "You will keep your lips zipped about Finn. As far as you're concerned, he's the man of my dreams. One I met a few months ago and haven't been able to pry myself away from since. And if hear any – and I do mean *any* – scintilla of a different story, I'll know where it came from. And you will regret it, Priscilla. I promise."

Priscilla narrowed her gaze; trying to figure out if she should call her bluff is what Farrah surmised. "Alright Farrah. Have it your way." *For now,* she added silently.

"Now that we're clear, fix that redness on your face. Then, let's link arms like the good friends we're supposed to be and go celebrate my ex-fiance's marriage," Farrah finished, her lips a straight line of defiance.

Chapter 14

“The pow-wow over,” Finn said, looking bemusedly from Farrah to Priscilla.

“Yes, we’re all caught up,” Farrah said, sending her friend a *‘don’t you forget what I just told you’* look.

Priscilla pursed her lips and tossed her blonde mane. She glued on a dazzling smile. “Yes, we are definitely all caught up.”

“We covered a lot of ground, but one thing we didn’t get around to is how you all met,” she said, letting the unspoken question hang in the air between Priscilla and Finn.

Before Finn could say anything, Priscilla jumped in. “You know I do some volunteer work at my friend’s gallery in Soho a couple of times a week. Finn walked in with one of his paintings one day.”

“How long ago was that?” Farrah asked, more curious than ever.

“Six, seven months. And the rest, as they say, is about to be history,” Priscilla said. “If you’ll excuse me,” she said, “I want to go catch up with Brynwen.”

“That Priscilla; she does have an eye for beauty,” Adelaide said, looking pointedly at Finn. “For art. She does,” Adelaide insisted, as innocently as a newborn babe.

Aaron colored.

Erica cleared her throat.

Farrah looked surprised.

Finn nodded in a ‘touche’ manner in Adelaide’s direction. He was sure everyone in the group knew a side of Priscilla that he didn’t. But that was conjecture for another day.

“I’m glad you all could come,” Adelaide said to the group, looking pointedly at Farrah. "Continue to enjoy yourselves. Excuse us while we check in on our other arriving guests" she said, leading Aaron away from the group.

"Must have been quite a row. She couldn't get away from you fast enough," Finn whispered into Farrah's ear when Adelaide and Aaron departed.

"We had some air to clear," Farrah admitted, excusing her and Finn away from the few others standing with them. The one thing she did like about his pretend-boyfriend status is that she didn't have to play games with him. She could be straightforward. It struck her how ridiculous it was that she could be totally honest with a stranger, but not the supposed love of her life.

It had taken her years to admit to Aaron that she really wanted to be married. And it had taken a few more years beyond that to admit to herself that she wanted a family. She had never told Aaron that, because she knew he wasn't keen on having children.

"Did you clear it?" Finn asked, as they sat on the bench where he and Adelaide had sat a little while earlier.

"Clear what?" Farrah asked.

"The air? With Priscilla?" Finn asked. The way he said Priscilla's name irked her. It sounded too intimate in his Irish lilt.

This day hadn't gone at all the way she wanted. Too many little bombshell surprises that were adding up to one big headache. Farrah rubbed her temples. "Yes, we cleared the air. We both know where we stand."

"That doesn't sound good," Finn said. "And you look like a stressed-out puss. I have a remedy for that," he said, the devil sparking in those blue eyes.

"You're here to help me win my fiance back, remember?"

"It's something I could hardly forget, considering how he's been ogling you since you got here." Finn returned. "But you also made me a promise sweet Farrah."

"What promise?"

"That you wouldn't cut me off from this prematurely," he said, his eyes sliding between her jean-clad legs as his right hand rested on a thigh.

Farrah could feel the heat of his hand through the thick fabric of her jeans.

"Remember?" Finn said, leaning into her. She could feel his breath on her lips.

"We are in public in case you forgot."

"I forget nothing when it comes to you," he said.

Farrah couldn't breath for a second. The words were so simple, but uttered so truthfully and so directly that they froze her.

Finn palmed the right side of her face. "I told you that I'd play my role perfectly. What could be more perfect than a man touching his woman?"

Damn he was good, Farrah thought. If this is how he pretended to be a lover, what was it like when he wasn't pretending. She wasn't sure her heart could take it.

Farrah licked her dry lips. "I--" She swallowed, wishing the croakiness in her voice away. "It's more than a little affection."

"Not where I come from. You Americans ... way too uptight?"

"You Europeans. Way too vulgar."

"That's not what you said a few days ago. And if I remember correctly, you were more than a little vulgar yourself."

"That was in the privacy of my bedroom," Farrah whispered. "And really, must you remind me of that right now?"

Finn chuckled, his hand sliding to the back of her neck. He massaged the softness there.

Farrah fought a purr of satisfaction.

"May you never be polite in bed Farrah Jane. Ever," he emphasized. "Now let's go upstairs. I really can help you get rid of that headache."

"I should probably hate you," Farrah said, as she noted more than a few eyes taking in their intimate display. She stood up to break the spell.

"There's a thin line between love and hate, Farrah Jane," he said, moving his hand up to encircle her waist.

Farrah pulled back from Finn, recalling one of her mother's favorite songs again. Twice in the last week she'd been reminded of a song she hadn't thought of in over two decades. It's almost like he could read her mind on some level.

Sweet Jesus, was she falling for her pretend boyfriend. He was acting. Acting! she reminded herself.

Finn reached for her again. "Are you okay? You're not going to faint on me, are you?"

Chapter 15

Finn applied just enough pressure to Farrah's neck and back to relax her muscles. It wasn't too hard like some of the expensive massage therapists she'd gone to. It was one of the reasons she wasn't keen on getting massages. But she could go for one of his any time.

"Oh my god you have no idea how good that feels," Farrah moaned into her pillow.

"Better?" Finn asked, as he continued to stroke her skin.

"You are full of surprises. That's not exactly what I expected when you said you could help me get rid of my headache."

"Disappointed?"

"A little," she smiled, turning her head to look at him. "But I'm glad the headache is gone. It was gearing up to be a bruiser."

"Glad to be of service. Now, do you want to talk about what happened with your friend?" Finn said, removing his hands from her. He lay on the bed beside her fully clothed, leaned against the massive mahogany headboard, and pulled her against the wall of his chest.

Farrah recalled their first morning together, when she'd lain in this exact position and traced circles on his naked chest. Had that really been only five days ago?

"We'll get to my so-called friend later. What I'm dying to know about right now is your living situation. You said you live in a van? Please tell me you're pulling my leg?"

"I'm not."

"But why? I don't understand."

Finn smiled. "I'm sure you don't, given the station in life you were born to."

"What's that supposed to mean?" Farrah said.

"Don't go giving yourself another headache," Finn chided. "I live in my van because I can't afford the rents in New York City. It's not rocket science."

"I'm guessing that kinda puts a damper on your dating life."

"Not necessarily. I've had quite a few move-in offers."

"I'm sure," Farrah said. Hell, she was tempted to take him in. The thought of bedding him every night was like a junkie to their drug of choice. Highly addicting. Impossible to refuse. Farrah shook her head to dismiss the thought.

"And you don't have a friend or relative or somebody you could stay with?"

"I don't believe in laying my head in places I can't afford to pay for."

"Pride goeth before the fall," Farrah said.

"Nothing to do with pride. It's just the way I was raised. My father always said, *'If you can't afford it, you don't need it.' It's* a life rule that's served me well."

"Everybody needs shelter," Farrah countered.

"I have shelter."

"You know what I mean."

"I do. But I disagree. Let me put it to you another way; a way you might understand better."

"I'm all ears," Farrah said.

Finn stuck a finger in her ear. "All the wax out. Ready to hear?"

Farrah giggled and pushed his hand away.

"You're so silly."

The light rumble of laughter in his chest echoed in her ear. He buried his hand in her hair, absently massaging her scalp.

Farrah closed her eyes as she listened to him.

"Living the way I do has allowed me to be free. I'm not chained to a job I hate wishing that someday I'd get to pursue what I love. I get to do what I love every day. I'll take living the way I do now, than having a traditional roof over my head doing what kills my soul day in and day out."

"That's sounds good in theory, but you're in your thirties now," Farrah said, opening her eyes as she began tracing circles on his chest again.

"What if things hadn't worked out? What about financial security? Having a wife? Children? Do you ever think about those things?"

"I take life as it comes Farrah. I want for nothing, and I have everything I need."

"How can you say that? You live in a van!"

Finn laughed. "Yes, I do."

"What are you smiling about? You're going on forty and you live in a van!" Farrah said, sitting up.

"The last time I checked, thirty-two was almost a decade away from forty.

Don't rush me woman!" he said, pulling her back down and dropping a kiss in the center of her forehead.

Farrah smiled at him and bit her bottom lip. "I'm sorry. I didn't mean-"

"It's ok."

"Can I ask you one more question?"

"Sure."

"Why do you really do it? I know what you just said, but you're resourceful enough to pursue your art and work a full-time job. If you wanted. I know it. So what made you make, what many would call, such an extreme choice?"

"It wasn't extreme for me. Life presents choices. You choose and you follow through until you decide to make other choices," he said, looking down at her.

"There's more to it than that. I don't know how I know, but I do. What is it, Finn?" Farrah said, sitting up so she could look at him squarely.

"Why do you want to know?" he said, hooding his eyes, which was all too easy to do with his ridiculously long lashes.

"Then it's true?" Farrah said.

"No one has ever pressed me for a reason."

"So are you going to tell me what it is?"

"How do you see me so clearly?" Finn asked. If he'd stopped to think about it, he never would have asked the question, but this woman – she pulled things out of him that even he'd forgotten was there.

"You let me," Farrah said simply.

At this, he lifted his lashes. He needed to see what she saw about him.

Farrah returned his gaze unflinchingly. He looked away. She lay her head back down on his chest. His heart beat in her ear, bringing a part of her to life. A part she didn't even know was there.

Five days. I've only known of this man's existence for five days.

"Where I come from in Ireland, it's the Ireland many think of when they see a postcard: rolling green hills; old stone buildings; endless clear lakes; lots of hole-in-the-wall pubs."

"Sounds heavenly," Farrah said.

"It is. But life there is very hard. It's just a small fishing village. No real industry. It's a place where you don't make a living so much as scratch one out. I'm an only child, which is unusual. My parents would have had more, but my father didn't believe in having more mouths to feed than he could afford. My mother didn't work. My father didn't believe that a woman should work outside the home. So he was the sole breadwinner. I didn't realize until I got older just how hard he struggled to keep food on the table for the three of us."

"You father sounds like a wise and very good man."

"He was, but he worked himself into an early grave."

"I'm sorry," Farrah said, planting a soft kiss on his chest. "How did he die?"

Finn ran his hand over the spot. The warmth of her lips on the cotton of his shirt a feeling he'd never forget. "Heart attack. He was night fishing. The old boat he had took on water when he was out in the lake. He managed to make it back to shore, but the doctor said the exertion was likely too much for him. A couple of his friends found him frozen to death on the bank of the river the next morning. I was grateful for that, because I'm not sure my mother could have survived not having a body to bury."

"How horrid."

"The hardest part was watching my mother blame herself. I knew what she was feeling because I blamed myself too."

"How old were you?"

"Twelve."

"And from that day on, you've been the man of the house and have assumed responsibility for your mother."

"Why would you say that?"

Farrah looked up at him. "Remember when you told me some feelings were universal?"

Finn nodded.

"Some reactions for certain kinds of people are universal. You were an only child; likely the apple of your father's eye. Of course you would want to take care of your mother."

"You see way too much Farrah Jane."

Farrah sighed, a small smile curving her lips. She could tell this was new territory for him; letting someone in. She cherished the feeling. "Continue, please," she said at his silence.

"You're right. I vowed then that I would take care of my mother; that she would one day have the easy life my father always wanted to give her – and me. So while I could well afford to find a place to live, I couldn't do that, pursue my career as an artist, and send money back to my mother. Something had to give."

"So you sacrificed a roof over your head to keep one over your mother's," Farrah stated. "And look at you. Now you're on your way," she said.

"Ah, the sweet luck of the Irish. I daresay it is with me." Finn said.

"Make light of it all you want, but if you hadn't met Priscilla--"

"If I hadn't met Priscilla, what? I'd be stuck in my van, practically homeless, another wannabe starving artist clogging up the streets of New York City? I've always been a survivor Farrah. That will never change."

He switched topics before Farrah could respond. "Tell me about Priscilla. Why is there bad blood between you? Is she going to keep your little secret?"

"It's not my little secret; it's our big secret. And as you're about to be famous, you'd better hope she does."

"I have a show. That's it. It could flop. Nothing ventured, nothing gained."

"Priscilla wouldn't have referred you to an agent if she thought your work was no good. If she says you have talent. You have talent. One thing I will give her is she knows art. And once you're known in the circles she runs in, you're on your way to being famous. Very famous. She knows the people who buy art. She knows the art critics. She knows the people who sit on the boards of art foundations and put together charity balls at the Met, the Guggenheim, the--"

"I get the picture," Finn said. "Priscilla's well connected."

"I was not prepared for this."

"For what?" Finn said.

"To answer questions about us, not beyond the little story we'd conjured up. Why did you have to be discovered now?" Farrah opined. She rolled off Finn's chest and onto her pillow, rubbing her trying-to-throb-again temple. "This is turning out to be a disaster."

"Slow down little one. You have nothing to worry about as long as I'm here," Finn reassured her. He reached down and cupped her face, pressing his lips to hers.

"Now tell me what about Priscilla upsets you so," he said, his hands lightly rubbing her temples. He felt almost guilty extracting information from her when she was obviously in such emotional turmoil. But he had to know about Priscilla. What signs had he missed that she was married? "You've obviously known each other a long time. Why are you more like enemies than friends?"

"It didn't use to be that way. We used to be so close."

"What happened?"

"According to her, I haven't been myself since Aaron and I split."

"And according to you?"

"I've been a wreck, I admit. But on some levels, I've felt more like myself than ever."

"Why?" Finn said, his hands moving down to her shoulders. Farrah moaned in relaxation. She loved the way he touched her.

"Priscilla's right. I'm not the same person as I was when I was with Aaron. I'm angrier and not quite so easy to mold. I push back more. I question more. ... And I hurt more," Farrah said, picking at non-existent lint on the bedding.

"Hurt how?" he said, noting her nervous picking.

"I'm adopted. I've never felt like I belonged in the world my adoptive parents raised me in. I've always felt like an impostor and that my parents and the Priscillas of the world let me live in their universe as long as I obeyed the rules; behaved myself, so to speak."

"What rules?" Finn asked.

Farrah remained quiet. She'd only explained how she felt about her parents to one other living soul. Aaron. She ran a hand along Finn's left forearm, which continued to massage her temples

She looked into his eyes. "Rules like join the right clubs. Go to the right schools. Date the right people. Play the right sports. The list goes on and on."

"Play the right sports?" Finn questioned.

"I know it may sound silly to someone like you. But trust me, when you're raised in that bubble and it's all you've ever known, it can be quite isolating if you don't conform."

"And you didn't conform?"

"I thought I did. The only rebellious thing I ever did was not marry right out of college. I know my parents expected grandchildren by now. I'm practically an old maid at thirty-one."

"Is this the twenty-first century, or the eighteenth?" Finn asked.

"In some social circles, things change very slowly. It's in the best interest of the status quo to keep it that way."

"I never would have dreamed that in a city like New York, such old-world rules still applied.

"Oh they do. Trust me they do," Farrah said. "I place a lot of the blame on women."

"Why?" Finn asked.

"Take Priscilla. She married right out of college. And she actually admitted that the reason she was getting married was because she liked not having to worry about things."

"But she's so intelligent?"

"Extremely. She could be rich in her own right if she wanted. It's a shame she didn't do more with her art history degree. She'd be a great gallery owner, which is why I know that if she says you have talent, you have talent."

So that part of her was real, Finn thought. Priscilla was being truthful when she told him she had a degree in art history and that she'd always had a love of the arts. He hadn't really doubted it, as her knowledge was evident within minutes of talking to her. The depth and breadth of it couldn't be faked. But he'd sense something was off with the leggy blonde a couple of months into dating her. He'd put it down to his living situation. That she could be married never crossed his mind.

"So why do you think she never put her degree to use? *Why make your own money when you can marry* it' is her logic. Priscilla comes from money, but not the kind of money her husband has. Her marriage is more of a business merger than a marriage. Her husband is the founder of a European hedge fund. They do a lot of business with her father's investment firm."

"Money begets money," Finn said.

"Exactly. I can't tell you how many marriages like that I know of. And and these are educated women who could do very well for themselves. But they marry, have children, and pass it along to the next generation."

"And that dream wasn't for you?"

"Not like that."

"Is that why you felt like you didn't belong?"

"Partly. But Aaron made it bearable. He reassured me that I belonged. So I didn't mind being in that bubble because he was in it. He said that as long as he had anything to say about it, no one would make me feel like I didn't belong."

"And did he keep that promise?" Finn asked.

"He did. Aaron has his flaws, but I never felt less than when I was with him. And that's how I knew he loved me. Everybody in my life who's supposed to love me has made me feel less than at some point. But not Aaron."

"Are you sure about that?"

"Yes," Farrah said. "Why would you doubt that?"

"I'm not trying to hurt you Farrah. I just want to be sure that you're seeing all of who he is," Finn said.

"I do. I know Aaron, maybe better than he knows himself."

"Then what was up with the remark about you 'carrying around a suitcase full of warpaint?' Not the nicest thing to say to someone you used to care deeply for, especially when you haven't seen them for months." *And why didn't he marry you to secure your place in your circle?* He wondered if Farrah had ever thought to ask herself that question.

"That's just Aaron. He can be a little passive aggressive, but it's nothing compared to some of the things some people have said to me, and about me. Trust me."

"Just because it's not as bad as things others have said, that makes it ok?"

"No. I mean yeah … I mean-- Look Finn, unless you're part of my world, you wouldn't understand. And you can't base your whole assessment of someone on one little thing."

"No wonder you were in that bar alone and so willing to take me home?"

"What does that mean?"

"That you were – are – starved for affection. And you're so far along the starvation chain you don't even realize you're starving."

"How dare you talk to me like that," Farrah said.

"Like what? Tell you the truth? Try to make you see that the man you profess to love fell hella short?" Finn said calmly.

"You don't understand," Farrah insisted.

"I understand all too well. But it' s your life. I'm just here to serve."

"And don't you forget it," Farrah huffed, putting on her haughtiest look as she untangled herself from him.

"You may be accustomed to being talked to in any manner Ms. Bryant. But I'm not."

"You're here because of me," Farrah pointed out.

"And I could just as easily leave because of you."

"And just how do you plan on getting back to the city? I drove, remember?"

"Getting a ride is the least of my worries. I'm sure one of your lady friends would oblige; perhaps even Priscilla." Finn felt guilty as soon as the words left his mouth. Farrah didn't know that he and Priscilla had been lovers, but he did. And that made it a very cheap shot.

The fact that she was throwing herself at some guy who wasn't worthy of her was making him crazy, he justified to himself. And *that* made him even angrier.

She got under his skin so bad she was making him violate long-held principles. Hell, he didn't even know her. Why should he care if she wanted to sign up for heartbreak all over again?

"Well you picked the right one for a ride," Farrah said, her anger rising at the mention of Priscilla's name. "She'd not only give you a ride back to the city to spite me, but she'd probably fuck your brains out on the side of the road on the way there."

Finn's face colored.

"Don't get all embarrassed on me now," Farrah said, noting the color in his sculpted cheeks.

"She's a married woman," Finn mumbled.

"Consider it your lucky day, Mr. O'Hare. You wouldn't have to feel guilty about it. You see, she's been married for nine years. And every damn one of them have been unhappy. Her husband is decades older and I bet she hasn't had a proper orgasm – at least from him – since the day she got married. And you're right up her alley. She'd fuck you in a heartbeat. But don't get any ideas about it being anything but. She'd never leave her husband. Even with your newfound fame, your earnings won't touch his. Her husband has more money than god. He's a frickin' billionaire – many times over."

"The games women play," Finn said, almost to himself.

"Some women," Farrah objected. "Not all of us play games."

Finn raised an eyebrow, as if to remind her how and why he came to be here with her.

"I'm not playing games," Farrah objected, reading his look. "And we were talking about Priscilla."

"Your game. Your rules," Finn said.

"Can this argument please be over?" Farrah said, her hands going to her temples again. "Fighting with a pretend boyfriend is just stupid."

"That's the first rational thing you've said in the last ten minutes," Finn said, his smile rupturing a vein in her heart. Now she truly knew what the term 'heart-stopping smile' meant.

"Come back here, woman," he said, pulling her to him.

Farrah didn't resist. "I can't wait to see your work," she said, her anger dissipating as quickly as it flared up, especially as she realized who she was angry with. Herself.

Farrah's inexplicably fast attachment to Finn was making it impossible to think clearly. She'd barely thought about Aaron when he wasn't right in front of her, never mind figured out what she wanted from this weekend.

"I thought we weren't going to be seeing each other after this weekend," Finn smiled.

"Who says we are? According to Priscilla, you're going to be having an art show. I definitely plan to attend. The curiosity is killing me."

"Then by all means, I'd love to see you there. Perhaps you'll bring your Aaron if you manage to steal him away from his bride-to-be this weekend."

"Perhaps," Farrah said, that dream taking a backseat to what she was feeling right now being in his arms.

"Perhaps Priscilla will take pity on me and make me her paramour for the evening."

"I highly doubt it. You live in a van. Priscilla is discerning. I don't think she'd take too kindly to your living situation."

She already had, Finn thought. She'd even offered to set him up in an apartment.

"Besides, she *and her husband* are great patrons of the arts. He'll be there on opening night with her, I'm sure. It's one of the few things they actually do together."

"You seem to know a lot about her marriage."

"We were close for a long time. Only the last couple of years have been rocky. ... If you're as talented as she says you are, I'm surprised she hasn't jumped your bones."

"Why would you say that?"

"There are two things that excite Priscilla besides money: discovering a new artist with real talent, and a gorgeous man. Her husband has the money. You have the other two things. In fact, you're just her type. I wasn't kidding about that."

"And what type is that?" Finn couldn't help but ask.

"Tall, dark, handsome, broody, talented, and seemingly aloof. ... Now that I think about it, it would surprise me if she hasn't tried to sleep with you. Did she?" Farrah asked.

"I never kiss and tell," Finn said, "Speaking of kissing," he said, grabbing her and burying his head in the curve of her neck.

That was her spot – the spot that drove her crazy. As he well knew.

"You are the only woman I want to sleep with right now." He hugged her tightly to him, his lips making dizzying circles on her soft flesh.

Farrah leaned into him, her eyes closed in flushed excitement.

His tongue worked its way around to her mouth, sliding into the warm cave as her breasts crushed against his chest, her whole body heaving in anticipation of the pleasure she knew was coming.

Her tongue fluttered against his as he laid her back on the bed, one hand buried in her hair as his mouth continued its totally welcome assault on hers.

She pulled him to her, delving her hands inside his shirt. The warm smoothness of his skin had her purring in his mouth.

"Slow down baby," he said, his blue eyes smoldering as he looked down at her.

"You feel so yummy," she said, her hands moving to his belt buckle. She deftly unfastened his pants, the sound of the zipper sliding down another instrument in their symphony of love-making.

"You're getting way too good at that," he teased.

"Watch my other skills," Farrah said brazenly, as she eased his jeans down. His cock sprang free.

She smiled, forgetting that he didn't wear underwear. She laughed as she brushed her lips against the smooth length of his swollen cock, palming it tightly.

Finn forced himself to remain still as his length melted into the sheath of her mouth. She gave a throaty laugh as she rolled her tongue from the base to the tip, then back again.

Finn dug his hands into her hair, controlling her motions as she nursed his cock to about-to-burst swollen-ness. His abs contracted, fighting for control. *Not again,* he thought. *She would not control his cock again.*

He snatched her head back, grabbed his dick and tapped it on her lips. "You like that, huh?"

"I love it," Farrah said, relishing the way he held her head back, a fistful of her hair in his hands.

"You little minx," Finn said, pushing her back down on the bed. "Now it's your turn to be tortured," he said, sliding one hand between her legs, as his lips devoured hers again.

He pushed her panties to one side and rubbed his cock against her moist slit.

Farrah tried to position herself for it to slide in, but he resisted her efforts, only letting tip dip in, before immediately pulling out again.

"That's not fair," she moaned.

"All's fair in war and fucking, Farrah Jane."

He planted one hard kiss on her lips, then nibbled his way down the rest of her body.

Farrah twisted and crooned her satisfaction, squeezing her eyes shut and losing herself in the pleasure zone of his lips.

All the muscles in her belly, thighs and hips quivered as his lips landed at the top of the soft flesh between her legs. Instinctively she opened wider, welcoming his warm tongue as it sliced it's way down her sacred center. He ripped her panties, tearing the seat of them before suctioning hard onto her jumping bud.

Farrah cried out her pleasure as his suctioned her juices, his tongue sinking deeply into her, then coming back and circling the sensitive skin of the inside of her womanhood. At the precipice of her orgasm, his lips released her, then slid two fingers in – softly at first, increasing the pace as her hips lifted up and down in concert with his fingers.

A strangled cry escaped Farrah as her head lobbed from side to side. He lowered his head and clasped tightly onto the crest of her womanhood. Her hips lifted off the bed as he suctioned it and circled his tongue over it again and again.

"Oh god, I'm coming," she announced. "I'm coming," she cried, fighting – not sure for what. To get away? To lean into the oblivion of her orgasm? To prolong it. To stop it. She didn't know, and she didn't care.

Finn clasped his hands over her upper thigh, holding her captive as he sucked her juices.

Farrah wound her hips round and round, her head thrashing back and forth as she gurgled and crashed her way into heaven.

Before she could recover, he eased himself up and plunged into her wetness.

She was so hot and wet that he stilled himself after the first thrust, knowing that if he slid into her exquisite tightness again, he would lose control and explode. And she felt too good for that. He'd waited four long days to be inside her again. He wasn't going to waste it like some schoolboy just getting his rocks off.

Farrah moaned, tightening her legs around him, urging him in again.

He kissed her, pleased that she wanted him as much as he wanted her. The kiss ignited a fire that roared through them, and Finn plunged in again – slowly, steadily, deeply. "Sweet, sweet, sweet Farrah," he whispered against her lips as he moved in her, just inside the line of control.

"Your fuck me so good," she whispered. "So so good," she repeated. Her hands slid down the smoothness of his back. "Fuck me Finn," she commanded, closing her beautiful brown eyes as her hips thrust themselves into him.

"Sweet Jesus of Mary," Finn declared, as he rode her.

He put both hand under her buttocks, and drove into her again. They were a mass of lips and hands and cock and tits and pussy. The room filled with the scent of lust as they drained each other, racing to the peak of pleasure.

His last thrust landed in the bottom of her. For a moment he felt stuck, suctioned deep inside a well that he never wanted to be free of.

Farrah cried out.

"Did I hurt you?" Finn said as pulled out.

Farrah bit his shoulder. "Yes. A little. And I look forward to you doing it again," she grinned.

"Sweet Jesus woman, you're trying to kill me," Finn said as she rolled over

on top of him.
***

Finn stared at the sleeping woman next to him. She was ravishingly beautiful in her sleep. It took everything in him not to wake her and take her again.

Instead he slid from the bed, put on his running clothes and slipped out of the room. This was getting much more complicated than he'd bargained for.

Maybe he was overthinking it. Maybe he'd just met his sexual match and that was it. Even as he formed the thought, his mind rejected it.

He looked at his watch. The festivities for the evening weren't scheduled for another two hours or so. Just in time to get in a long run and clear his head.

He planted a kiss on her cheek on his way out.

He could feel the velvet of her skin on his lips as the late summer breeze floated across his heated skin.

Chapter 16

Finn picked up pace along the deserted trail – almost as if he was trying to outrun his persistent thoughts.

He wanted to see Farrah again after this weekend, but she'd made it clear that she was still in love with her ex. Her body's response to him told another story though. He wondered how she could give herself to him so freely, yet profess her love for another? It didn't make sense – and the very contradictory nature of her only made him want her more. She was everything he knew he shouldn't want, but everything he was coming to believe he'd give a great deal to have.

And then there was Priscilla. She'd played him – good. He was less angry about that though than the conundrum it put him in with Farrah.

Farrah didn't realize it yet, but after speaking with Adelaide, he knew it wasn't going to work out for her with Aaron. Adelaide was almost manic about her soon to be husband. She wasn't about to let him go under any circumstance. And Aaron, the poor sod, he was too weak of a man to override her insistence. Finn was sure of that because otherwise, Aaron never would have let himself get roped into marrying Adelaide. He didn't love her, that was obvious. And he wasn't in love with Farrah either. He desired her. But he definitely didn't love her, or he never would have left her.

He hadn't had the heart to tell Farrah any of this though. Better for her to find out on her own. And, he'd be there to pick up the pieces. But how far could he get with her without telling her about Priscilla?

Dammit, how could one great night of sex lead to so many problems! In a city of over eight and a half million people, he had to meet and fuck two friends. What were the chances?

"With that kind of luck, I should probably buy a fucking lottery ticket?"

Finn huffed, as he came to a stop.

Usually by the end of a long, hard run, he had an answer to whatever problem was rattling around his head. Not this time. If anything, he was more confused than ever – and he had to take a wicked piss.

He veered off the path and ducked behind an old barn. As he emptied his bladder, he heard an unmistakable voice.

***

"Oh god, yes, yes, yes! Yeeessss," the woman screamed.

A male voice growled in tune with a slapping sound.

Finn grinned as his long horse piss continued. Nothing brings out lovers like a wedding, he surmised.

"Sh… shit … shheeeit!" the man said, pumping faster.

"Harder baby. Harder!" the woman demanded.

Finn froze. He recognized that voice. He inched closer to the barn and peeked through a wooden slit in the back of a horse stall.

A sheath of blonde hair hung over the shoulder of a petite woman as a man slammed into her from behind. The man's knees buckled in orgasm.

Finn felt bile rise in his throat. He leaned back against the side of the barn, willing the rush of blood from his ears as the lovers finished their frenzied fuck.

"Damn baby, that was quite the goodbye session."

"Is it really goodbye? You've tried to cut me off before, but you always come back," Aaron said, easing out of Priscilla.

"Not this time Aaron. This time it really is goodbye. I'm in love with Finn," Priscilla declared, her bare bottom on a bale of hay as she slipped on her underwear.

Aaron laughed. "I think Farrah might have something to say about that."

"What's so funny? And no she won't?" Priscilla declared.

"You and this notion of love. We've been doing this," Aaron said, referring to their sexual relationship, "for how long? And how many lovers have you had over the years since you've been married? I don't think you're capable of love Prissy."

"Just sucker punch me in the gut, why don't you? That's cruel Aaron. All human beings are capable of love."

"I'm not trying to hurt you sweetheart. It's just that I know you – probably better than anyone in the world. And love has never been your thing."

"All the more reason you should believe me when I tell you that I've found it."

"Then what are you doing here trying to fuck my brains out?"

"You don't have to be crass," Priscilla said, hiding her hurt behind a cascade of hair. "But if you must know, it's be … because I needed to feel close to someone," she said, tears moistening her sea-green eyes. She tucked her hair behind her left ear. "Seeing Finn with Farrah caught me by surprise.

It hurt. A lot.”

“They really seem to be hot and heavy. The way he looks at her, I have to admit, I didn’t like it.”

“You dumped Farrah almost six months ago and you’re about to be married. Why do you care how another man looks at her?”

“It’s a man thing. Once we’ve had you, we always feel like you can have you.”

“You don’t say,” Priscilla said, rolling her eyes at the chauvinistic notion. *Men, they really were the dafter sex!*

“It’s true; a little secret from the man book that I’ll deny on a stack of bibles if you tell anyone I said it.”

Priscilla’s mouth curved into a smile; one that disappeared as quickly as it had appeared. “You ever think you made a mistake letting Farrah go?”

“I know I did,” Aaron said, to Priscilla’s surprise.

Finn’s brows knitted together in a flash of anger. And curiosity.

“Then why didn’t you go back to her?”

“I’d already been involved with Adelaide a few months before I left Farrah. Adelaide expected a proposal. I couldn't string her along.”

“You mean like you did Farrah?”

“Yes,” Aaron said, his affirmation tinged with guilt.

“Like you Prissy, I decided to do the smart thing and marry – since I had to – for money.”

“Why do you have to get married?” Priscilla asked.

“To get my inheritance. My father has made it very clear that if there are no grandchildren, preferably an Aaron LeGrew Montblanc, IV, there will be significantly less coming to me as I wouldn’t need it since I’m not carrying on a legacy. *If you choose to go it alone my boy, I’ll leave most of your share to where it can do some good.* Those were his exact words.”

“So why didn’t you just marry Farrah? She was crazy in love with you. And she would have gladly given you a kid or two.”

“Marrying Farrah never could have happened. My father would have cut me out of his will for good.”

“But you were with her for almost an entire decade,” Priscilla said, confused.

“Exactly. And my father made it clear that it was time to make a decision about what I wanted -- her or my inheritance. And my inheritance comes with strings. Farrah was fine as a girlfriend, but not as a wife or mother of future Montblancs.”

“You mean he’s Meghan Markle-ing you? How royally fucked up that is,” Priscilla said. “Does Farrah know?”

“No. She thinks my parents loved her. And they do, just not in that role. So I figured it this way, if my father gets any other notions about cutting me out of his will – say, for example, if I decided not to procreate – I’ll have

Adelaide."

"You mean Adelaide's money," Priscilla clarified.

"If you must be so vulgar," Aaron said. "She's a perfectly lovely woman. And the fact that she comes from more money than the Rockefellers and Vanderbilts combined doesn't hurt."

"I never knew your folks were that cold. I truly thought they accepted Farrah."

"They did. They do — as someone else's wife. Not mine."

Priscilla thought back to what Farrah had accused her of. Had she mistreated her friend without knowing it? She never would have guessed that Aaron's folks would disapprove of him marrying Farrah. But Farrah had professed to always feeling like an outsider. Were the people in their world so good at hiding their true feelings that one of their own — her — didn't recognize it? Who else felt that way? Her parents? Her godfather? Brynwen's parents? Her world couldn't all be an illusion, could it?

"I think on some level Farrah did know Aaron," Priscilla said.

"I think so too," Aaron said. "Another reason it was best to let her go. I always hated that she felt like an outsider. She has more class and manners than most of the no-brain twits from the so-called best families."

"You really loved her," Priscilla said.

"I did, but she deserved better. She would have left me eventually anyway."

"I'm not so sure about that," Priscilla said.

"Farrah's a smart woman. I'm sure she would have."

"I can tell you from first-hand experience that just because a woman is smart does not mean she applies that to her love life. Farrah's still in love with you Aaron," Priscilla said.

"Not from the way she looked at that Irishman. She seems positively loopy for him," he said, annoyed at the thought.

"There's nothing between her and Finn."

"Were we watching the same two people? Just because you may have boned him for a few months doesn't mean that he's not serious about her."

"He's not."

"You sound so sure. How do you know?"

"Because she met him in a bar not even a week ago. Apparently she took him home, fucked his brains out and got the idea to bring him here to make you jealous. He's her, shall we say, stand-in lover."

"You joshing me," Aaron said, stupefied.

"I don't josh; you know that."

"I had no idea she still carried such a torch for me."

"Would it have made a difference?" Priscilla asked.

"Probably not. I truly hoped that she'd moved on; although seeing her did mess with me a bit. Farrah's not the kind of woman a man easily forgets."

"You loved her but you let her go. Makes me wonder if you really loved her. Feeling what I do for Finn, I could never let him go."

"Sometimes you don't deserve the thing you love. Farrah's special. We wanted different things out of life. If I didn't care, I would have kept her."

"You forget who you're talking to Aaron. You let Farrah go because you had to fully bag Adelaide."

"Ok. That, *and* I felt guilty about cheating on her and lying to her."

"It didn't stop you from sleeping with me. And I'm her friend. So just how deeply could you have loved her?" Priscilla pointed out.

"We've been sleeping with each other for so long, I don't even think of it as cheating," Aaron said.

"That's the Aaron I know and love," Priscilla said, batting his hand away from an exposed breast. "This was one for the road, remember? And we've come to the end of our road Aaron. I mean it."

"Sorry. Old habits are hard to break. Now that you're leaving my lover's nest, maybe Farrah can take your place, become my *de facto* lover. Maybe I *can* have my cake and eat it too."

Finn fists curled into twin balls of rage. *The bastard!*

"You're not serious!" Priscilla said. "For one, Farrah would never go for it. And two, why don't you finally grow up Aaron? Be a real husband to Adelaide. A faithful husband. You all have enough in common. She could make you happy if you'd give her a chance."

"Not in the cards, my dear," Aaron said, unphased by Priscilla's sudden flash of anger. And while he hadn't been serious about taking Farrah as a lover, the more he thought about it, the more it appealed to him for one reason. Farrah made his dick hard. His fiance didn't. And now that Priscilla was ostensibly going to be unavailable, who was he going to turn to when he wanted a reliably good fuck.

He could always pay for it, but that didn't appeal to him for an all-the-time thing. He liked the familiarity of sleeping with someone he knew, and someone who knew him. That's why he and Priscilla had lasted so long. They'd been hooking up since high school.

And Farrah – she was even more beautiful than he remembered and they'd always had a special kind of sexual energy. Screwing Priscilla was more rote; it got him off when he was horny and they could laugh and talk to each other. But Farrah; there was a different kind of chemistry there. He knew he would never tire of her.

Farrah just might be the answer he was looking for. She just might make this new marriage he wasn't looking forward to more tolerable. He'd be good to her – better than good. She'd never want for anything; he could see that she progressed in her career faster than she could ever do for herself, and he'd do his darnedest to be faithful to her. Outside of his wife, of course.

Maybe, just maybe, her being here was the answer to his prayers.

"Aaron!" Priscilla whispered, tugging on his arm. "Didn't you hear me?" she asked as he turned to her.

"What? And why are you whispering?" Aaron said, running his hand across his chin as he thought about the soft hairs between Farrah's legs. He'd always loved sliding his tongue in her. Her slim hips would jack knife off the bed as she groaned his name.

"I think I heard someone," Priscilla whispered, putting her hand to her lips to signal to him to be quiet.

Finn froze beside the barn. If they came out, there'd be nowhere for him to hide. He had no idea how he'd explain his presence there. This could turn into a shitfest, he thought. And Farrah was smack dab in the middle.

"I don't hear anything," Aaron said, after a few seconds. This is a barn. It's probably just field mice in some haystacks."

"I guess you're right," Priscilla agreed after not hearing any more noises. "Or it's my guilty conscious messing with me. Let's get out of here."

Finn prayed for the third or fourth time in as many minutes that they didn't exit just yet. He started to ease to the closest corner of the barn so he could re-enter the trail he'd been running on before they spotted him.

"Not before you tell me more about you and this Finn character," Aaron returned. "What's so special about him that's got you thinking you're in love. I know you've always had a thing for artists, but--"

Finn froze.

"You know how you said Farrah was special?" Priscilla interjected.

Aaron nodded his head.

"That's how I feel about Finn. I've never felt like this before. As much as I hate to admit it, you were right; I had come to believe that I wasn't made to fall in love. But I knew I was in love with Finn when I decided to leave my husband."

"You left your husband?" Aaron said, shocked.

"Not yet," Priscilla said. "I'm planning my exit."

Finn's brow furrowed. At least what they had shared was real in some respect, he thought.

"Have you lost your feckless mind Prissy?! You'll regret it."

"No, I won't. I can't live without him Aaron," Priscilla said, tearing up. "I won't. I don't care what it costs. All I know is life doesn't make sense without him."

"You're serious," Aaron said.

"Yes. I already consulted a lawyer about filing for divorce."

"I guess the only constant in life is change," Aaron said. "I'm getting married and you're filing for divorce. The world really is upside down," Aaron said.

Priscilla smiled. "It's really is the end of an era, huh?"

"I guess it is."

"You ought to rethink your marriage to Adelaide, Aaron. She's a good woman, and she happens to be crazy about you."

"I know, but the only thing I can promise is that I'll be discreet. I'm under no illusions about remaining faithful to Adelaide. I don't think having sex with one woman for the rest of my life is in my genes. Two maybe," he said, thinking of Farrah. "But not one – especially one I'm not particularly attracted to"

Would Farrah agree to be his mistress, he pondered. If she's been carrying a torch for him since they split, maybe he had a shot.

"If Adelaide finds out that you're fucking around on her, she might have you castrated," Priscilla joked, breaking through the sudden daydream that Aaron wanted to make a reality more and more.

"Farrah never found out, and we were together for almost ten years. I think I know how to play this game. Almost as well as you, my sweet," Aaron quipped.

"I finally met someone I don't want to play games with. I love Finn Aaron, and I'm willing to give up everything to be with him. I have to make him see that."

"He'd be a fool if he didn't," Aaron said, kissing Priscilla on the forehead.

"Thanks for that," Priscilla said, looping her arm through Aaron's like the old friends they were.

"What are you going to do about Farrah?" Priscilla asked.

"Perhaps she'll become my next conquest since I'll no longer have access to your delectable-ness," Aaron said, masking his seriousness with a mischievous chuckle. Bedding Farrah regularly again would be a *coup de gras* even his already swollen ego would puff up at even more.

"I don't think you have the guts to go after her," Priscilla said. "Although, it would suit my purposes just fine, especially if Finn is even remotely attached to her." As she feared. She'd seen the looks between Farrah and Finn too. And although she didn't want to admit it, Aaron had been right when he alluded to the fact that there was something there.

"She is still in love with me. Thanks to your sharing of that little piece of knowledge, I'd say I have a better than average chance," Aaron said, already thinking of his approach. "She'll be my wedding gift to myself," he mused, convincing himself that Farrah would be his again.

Finn let out the breath he didn't know he'd been holding as he watched the couple exit the barn.

Farrah. What in hell had she ever seen in that poke-any-hole-you can asshole?

And what the hell had he ever seen in Priscilla?

The pain in his knuckles alerted him to his hands. He unballed the fists he'd been tightening for the last fifteen minutes. The blood rushed down the tentacles of his hands at about the same rate it drained from his face.

As he made his way back to the mansion, he wished to God he'd held his piss.

Chapter 17

"Finn. Finn," Farrah called, wiping sleep from her eyes. She lay there for a few minutes, thinking back over the events of the last few hours. Being back among all of her friends felt strange. While there were some she was glad to see, like Brynwen, she felt more like an outsider than ever. Yet Aaron, as always, fit perfectly. She'd forgotten just how boastful and passive aggressive he could be. She immediately compared him to Finn, who was the exact opposite. He said what he meant and meant what he said. There were no hidden agendas; no societal codes to decipher.

He lives in a van, her brain screamed.

And yet, he occupied a mansion in her head.

***

Farrah checked her watch, surprised that she'd been asleep for well over an hour. She finally swung her legs out of bed. She made her way to the bathroom and switched on the shower.

Catching sight of herself in the mirror, she almost didn't recognize the sated expression looking back at her. An unbidden smile came to her lips as she felt the slight soreness between her thighs. Her face told a different story than the war raging within. How could her exterior look so right, when everything inside felt so wrong?

As she slowly removed her make-up, Priscilla's words haunted her all over again. *Ever since you and Aaron broke up, you've become little more than a ... well a common, loose woman. You need to get control of yourself; get control of your life.*

"What the hell are you doing Farrah?" she said to herself. Sleeping with one man while professing love for another. It was the antithesis of who she was, and yet ...

A knock sounded on the door. She slipped on her short silk robe, pulling the belt tight around her waist as she made her way to it.
"Who is it?"
"Aaron."

Chapter 18

"No time like the present," Priscilla said to herself, watching Aaron's back as he continued around to the front of the mansion.

She'd elected to enter the house from the rear and take the back staircase to her bedroom suite. Even though no one would think twice about seeing her and Aaron together, now that the physical part of their relationship was over, she didn't want to risk unnecessary gossip. Now that she knew exactly what she wanted, her future was too promising for that.

She felt strangely free, yet terrified. For the first time in her life, she was going to do what wasn't expected of her. She was going to seek real happiness on her own terms. One thing she'd always admired about Farrah is that she'd followed that path right out of college.

"Priscilla," Adelaide called, as Priscilla put one foot on the first step of the staircase.

Priscilla jumped.

"I didn't mean to frighten you," Adelaide said.

Priscilla swallowed. "It's okay," she said, willing guilty color out of her cheeks and shame from her posture. She faced Aaron's soon-to-be wife, her brown hair sporting a pixie cut. With striking blue eyes and full lips, she somehow just missed being attractive. *The haircut,* Priscilla thought. *She had beautiful eyes. If she grew her hair out and went with an elongated bang, it would do wonders for her face.*

"I've been looking all over for you," Adelaide smiled, stopping Priscilla's silent assessment of her. "I need to speak with you. ... privately," she added as she started up the stairs.

Chapter 19

Finn tried to make sense of what he'd discovered about his and Farrah's ex. Lovers. For years. This weekend got stranger by the minute.

A bright spot of discovering this info was that it solved his conundrum with Farrah. All he had to do was tell her about Aaron and Priscilla, and she wouldn't want anything to do with either one of them again. He felt pretty sure of that.

However, it presented another problem. As much as he'd love for Farrah to find out what exactly what kind of scum her ex was, he couldn't bring himself to hurt her by telling her. This left him no closer to a realistic solution. How could he convince her that Aaron was not the man for her. *And perhaps convince her that he was?*

"What a fucking mess!" he hissed to to the surrounding nature. Like a boxer in training, Finn punched his left fist into his right hand. It was almost as if he was trying to pound an answer out of himself. *What should he do?* His thoughts tortured him as the back of the mansion came into view.

Thoughts of Farrah flooded him. Maybe he should just forget her. Lord knows he had enough on his plate these days. But then he thought about Monday. And the reality of never seeing her again caused a rebellion at the cellular level of his body. The thought of reducing what was going on between them to a few quick fucks after meeting in a bar – it was vulgar.

While he couldn't put a title on what was between them, he knew it was nowhere near vulgar. And maybe that's why he hadn't allowed himself to examine what it was. Because it was too powerful, too transformative to explain with a mere tag – boyfriend, girlfriend, lover.

All he knew was that this weekend was not enough. Being with her felt like the light his soul had been bending towards since he'd been born. He couldn't let that go. He wouldn't. And the reality of that stopped him in his tracks. How was he going to move forward with her, when her heart wanted another?

Finn looked up, pinpointing the window to their room, where he'd left her sleeping. It had been all he could do to walk out the door without taking her again. His manhood got hard just thinking about the smoothness of her skin and the way she bit her bottom lip when she smiled up at him from beneath him.

"That's it!" he said, pounding his fist one last time. There was no law written that he had to do anything – at least not immediately. For now, he'd he'd communicate with her in the one language they both intuitively understood – sex.

Once that no-good fecker of an ex was married, he knew Farrah would never pursue him. Then, he could start his pursuit of her in earnest.

Finn started a slow trot again, eager to bury himself in her once again.

His phone rang. He stopped and pulled it from the pocket of his running jacket. He saw the name and nervously punched the answer button.

Chapter 20

"Even with no make-up, you always were fetching," Aaron said as he entered the room, noting the smooth richness of Farrah's skin in the little white silk robe she had fastened about her.

She closed the door behind him, noting once again how somehow he always managed to give backhand compliments. *Finn would have just called her fetching,* she thought.

"Surprised?" he asked.

Farrah shook her head, not trusting her voice to speak. Surprise was an understatement. It had been almost six months since they'd been alone together. She thought back to the last time. It was the morning he had left her. They'd made love, she remembered. He'd been rushed, distracted. She thought it was because he had a lot going on at his new job with Fulbright technologies; a position he'd secured about a month before he left he. It was with his bride-to-be's father's company.

Weeks later, Farrah had read about his engagement in the *Weddings and Engagements* section of *The New York Times*. Strangely enough, Priscilla had been the one to call and tell her about it; telling her that she didn't want her to stumble upon it, or hear it from someone else.

The wedding was just months away. So not only was Aaron getting married, he was apparently eager to do so. The knowledge had sliced Farrah to the white-meat of her bones. And she still hadn't healed; her heart a giant scab she hoped no one noticed.

"Cat got your tongue?" Aaron said, his hands in his pockets as he leaned against the door she'd just closed.

"Huh?" Farrah said, snatching herself from the pain of her too-recent past.

"I asked if you were surprised that I'm here."

"Yes, very," Farrah answered as she wrapped her arms around herself. She felt, strangely, too exposed in her short silk robe.

"Why?" Aaron asked.

"I think the answer is obvious."

"Be that as it may, why don't you tell me anyway."

"You're about to be a married man Aaron. I don't think your bride-to-be would be thrilled that you're in a bedroom with your ex-fiance."

"Adelaide trusts me."

"Just like I did," Farrah pointed out. "But you left me. And you wasted no time moving on, obviously. Why Aaron?" Farrah said, her voice shaking, but forthright. "You didn't have to leave me like that."

Farrah surprised herself by asking the question she'd wanted to ask for months. She hadn't pictured it coming so easily. She'd imagined herself asking in anger, with tears, in desperation. But she'd never felt more calm. *Strange,* she thought, assessing her emotions as she looked at him leaning so casually against the door.

Farrah went to sit on the bed. She sat Indian-style, fondling the belt of her silk robe as her gaze held his. This was another surprise. She thought she'd be too angry or too desperately in love to look him directly in the eye for fear that he'd see how badly he'd hurt her.

"Does it really matter why I left? Looks like you've moved on too," Aaron said, feeling her out. His eyes were glued to the hand she used to push a haven of hair behind one ear. He'd forgotten how delicately beautiful her hands were. But he hadn't forgotten how they'd felt wrapped around his cock as she eased it into her mouth. She gave some of the best head he'd ever had. He willed his dick not to rise. At least not yet.

Why the hell had he let her go!

"Looks can be deceiving," Farrah said, regretting the words as soon as they were out. But it was the truth. She decided to let it stand; not try to cover up her truth.

Aaron thought back to what Priscilla had told him. Even though he believed her, he also knew what his eyes had seen between Farrah and the Irishman. But here she was before him, cool as a cucumber. Was that disinterest? Or, was she hiding her feelings from him? He pushed to find out.

"So you're not in love with the Irishman?" Aaron smiled.

"What do you want Aaron?" Farrah asked evasively. "Why are you really here?"

"What if I said I made a mistake letting you go?"

"Wh—what do you mean?" Farrah asked, not believing her ears. *He did not just say that? Did he?* Her heart rate picked up speed.

"What if I said I know it was a mistake to let you go?" he continued, walking over to the bed to sit beside her. He took one of her hands in his.

"That doesn't make any sense," Farrah said, almost to herself. His declaration totally threw her off balance. It was the last thing she expected. The very last. She looked at her hand in his. His touch. She'd dreamed about it for months. But she pulled away. "Adelaide?"

"What doesn't make any sense?" Aaron asked, as he reached for her hand again, and completely ignored the mention of his fiance.

"This. You. Me. What you're saying?"

"So what Priscilla said isn't true?" Aaron said, deciding to confront her with her own feelings.

"What did she say?" Farrah asked.

"That you're still carrying a torch for me. Is it true Farrah? Are you still in love with me?"

Chapter 21

Priscilla put on her brightest smile as she took a seat on the large settee in the sitting room adjoining Adelaide's bedroom.

So this is what guilt feels like, Priscilla thought, as her heart skittered around her chest. There was nothing in Adelaide's demeanor that said she knew about her dalliances with Aaron. The young woman had even smiled down at her on the staircase when she'd invited her to this little tete-a-tete. But, she felt guilty nonetheless.

"What can I do for the bride to be?" Priscilla said, needing to speak in order to calm her usually rock-steady nerves.

"You can stop sleeping with Aaron," Adelaide said, the smile on her face never slipping. "Correction. You *will* stop sleeping with him."

Adelaide's smile finally vanished.

"Wh-what do you mean?" Priscilla stammered.

"I know I may appear clueless where my soon-to-be husband is concerned. But I assure you, I'm not."

"Bu-but," Priscilla continued to stammer.

"Do us both a favor and don't deny that the two of you are lovers. I don't know when it started, and I don't care. But it will stop."

Priscilla wiped her brow.

Adelaide passed a tissue across the one cushion separating them on the three-pillowed, antique settee.

"I had hoped that Aaron had gotten his philandering ways out of his system. And to be perfectly honest, I expected to find him twisted up under Farrah's skirts this weekend. Alas, the *who* doesn't matter. The only thing that matters is the what, which is that I know Aaron is prone to affairs. He can't keep his pecker in his pants, as my grandmother would say."

Was that a giggle she just heard, Priscilla thought, crossing her brows in a cauldron of confusion. She wanted to laugh out loud at the absurdity of the situation, but knew she didn't dare. She struggled to keep her jaw from flying apart as Adelaide continued.

"The day after tomorrow, Aaron will become my husband. And he will be a faithful husband."

At that, Priscilla's jaw did open.

"Trust me dear, he will," Adelaide declared. "I just wanted you to know that I know what's been going on between you two, and that this afternoon was your last, shall we say, indiscretion. Are we clear?"

Priscilla shook her head. No one wanted to be on the wrong side of a Fulbright. Her husband may have more money, but the Fulbrights had more power. Power always trumped money. Always. So if she'd had any doubts about her affair with Aaron being over, this put the nail in the coffin. And she couldn't have been more pleased. She was ready to turn the page.

"Can I ask you a question?" Priscilla ventured. The tissue Adelaide had passed to her became a ball of white in her sweaty, left palm.

"Anything," Adelaide said, smoothing out the crisp poplin of her light-blue dress.

Her calm acceptance of the situation was unnerving for Priscilla. Tears she could deal with. This almost zen-like acceptance, on the other hand, was almost frightening.

Priscilla swallowed. "Why have you never said anything? If you know Aaron's, his uhm, ah ..."

"Proclivities," Adelaide supplied, as Priscilla struggled to land on the right word.

"Proclivities," Priscilla repeated, "why do you want to marry him?"

"It's quite simple really. I love him."

"At the risk of getting too personal," Priscilla continued, "you do know it's going to be a full-time job getting Aaron to keep his pecker in his pants?"

Adelaide laughed at Priscilla's use of her grandmother's turn of phrase.

Priscilla pressed. "Why would you sign up for that? You can have practically any man you want."

"Thank you for saying that. But it's precisely because I know *why* I can have any man I want that I've selected Aaron."

"I don't understand," Priscilla said.

Adelaide continued. "I'm not a raving beauty like you or Farrah. Most of the men I'm attracted to will only be with me because of who I am. They wouldn't look twice at me if I wasn't a Fulbright."

Priscilla colored. She'd walked right into this awkward observation. "I didn't mean ...

Adelaide held up a hand to stop her. "I accepted that truth a long time ago – somewhere around middle school. A girl's first crush can teach her lifelong lessons.”

“First crush?,” Priscilla echoed.

“I was twelve when I had my first one. He was gorgeous. Dark-brown, wavy hair. Green eyes; much like the color of yours. He was thirteen, but could have easily passed for sixteen or seventeen because he was tall and already had a filled-out body; not gangly like a lot of twelve and thirteen-year-olds. Even today, I still swoon when I think of him.”

“Sounds like he would have made a lot of girls swoon.”

“He did,” Adelaide laughed.

“We had a Sadie Hawkins dance coming up, and I had decided that I was going to ask him to go with me. My mother said, *Don’t you think you should aim a little lower?’* I didn’t understand at the time, but what I came to understand soon thereafter was the he was out of my dating league, so to speak.”

Priscilla couldn’t relate, as she had been the female equivalent of Adelaide’s object of affection – beautiful, popular, physically mature, and sought-after. She felt sorry for the young Adelaide. “Did you ever ask him?” she asked.

“Yes. And he accepted.”

“That’s great,” Priscilla said.

“I thought so too. Until I caught him making out with the gorgeous French exchange student. Do you know who Jacqueline Bisset is?”

Priscilla nodded her head.

“That’s who the exchange student looked like; like her in her prime.”

“Whew,” Priscilla whispered. “That’s some stiff competition.”

“Exactly,” Adelaide said. “I stood them watching them make out for I don’t know how long. It could have been five seconds or five minutes. All I know is, when they finally did came up for air, she asked him why he hadn’t gone with her to the dance. He told her that I’d asked first, and that his parents told him that nobody turns down a Fulbright. Not even an ugly one like me because life is all about connections, and the sooner he could start forming them, the better.”

“That must have been very painful,” Priscilla said slowly, feeling even more guilty about her dalliances with Aaron since he’d been engaged to Adelaide. She was even more happy that that part of her life was over.

“It was. I must have cried for a week. But, it was a life lesson I never forgot. My therapist tells me that was a turning point for me. I don't know about that, but what I do know is, once I started thinking about marriage, I figured I’d marry someone I loved and was attracted to. One-sided love is better than no love at all,” she said, almost wistfully.

“Even if that means marrying someone who only wants you for your money,” Priscilla said, rushing to add, “Not that I’m saying that’s the case with Aaron.”

"As I said, my eyes are wide open where my fiance is concerned, Priscilla. … Wealth is a great equalizer. As I see it, if you can't buy yourself the husband you are crazy about, what good is money – especially when you tend to date out of your league. I'm attractive enough and rich enough that Aaron will behave himself. Or, I'll take distinct pleasure in making sure he regrets it for the rest of his life."

Priscilla's eyes widened, but she remained quiet.

"I've never told anyone that story but my therapist. So if I hear it repeated, I'll know from whom it came," she warned, her smile as perfect as if they'd been discussing wedding china.

There was that knife in velvet gloves look again, Priscilla thought. She wondered if Aaron knew exactly who he was marrying. And if he didn't figure it out soon, she pitied the price he'd pay when he did.

***

Priscilla heaved a sigh of relief as she hurried down the hall to her suite of rooms to get dressed for the evening's festivities. Her chat with Adelaide had unsettled her. It solidified that she made the right decision where Aaron was concerned.

A life with Finn was what she wanted. Now, all she had to do was find a way to pry Farrah's hooks out of him.

And get hers back in.

Chapter 22

"I have to go get dressed for dinner," Finn said to his agent. He looked at his watch. The conversation had been going on for almost half an hour. He had just about twenty-five minutes to get dressed for the dinner party the bride and groom were hosting for their guests this evening.

This should be interesting, he thought. He couldn't believe all that had occurred in the four hours since he and Farrah had arrived.

He'd found out that Farrah's ex was a snake who couldn't keep it in his pants.

He'd found out that he'd been fucking one of her best friends.

He'd found out that he'd gotten the biggest break of his career.

He'd found out that Farrah's ex-fiance's soon-to-be wife was quite likable, and quite possibly had psychopathic tendencies.

But most importantly, he'd found out that he wasn't ready to let Farrah go.

What he hadn't figured out was how he was going to make her see that there was something that drew them to each other. And, that they deserved a chance to figure out what that was.

"Finn, are you there?"

"Yes, I'm here," he said to his agent.

"And there's absolutely no way you can make it back to the city by Sunday?"

"If you had told me that it couldn't wait til Monday, I would have said yes. But the wedding is Sunday. I'll see you bright and early Monday morning."

"If you weren't so talented Mr. O'Hare, this would be unacceptable."

"Then lucky for me, I am, in your words, 'the artistic find of the century,'" Finn returned jokingly.

"Sometimes I wonder why I do what I do," his agent replied

"Because you're brilliant at it," Finn replied. "See you Monday," he grinned as he hung up.

Even though his agent was way too flamboyant for Finn's liking, he had quickly come to have great respect for him. He was as brilliant as he was flamboyant, and this phone called had proven it.

His upcoming show was almost sold out. His agent had done a round of private pre-opening showings, and he was 'every bit as magnificent as I thought you were,' in the words of his agent. Patrons couldn't get enough of his work, and his agent wanted to discuss adding more pieces to the upcoming show.

He was still wrapping his head around the mind-boggling numbers that were thrown at him. His mother's future was secure. He couldn't wait to share the news with her … and Farrah.

Chapter 23

“Give you another chance?” Farrah said, looking at her ex-fiance as if he was speaking a foreign language.

“Yes,” Aaron said.

“Just like that?” Farrah said, snapping her fingers. The one question she’d thought would bring her so much joy made her inexplicably angry. “No explanation for why you left me like you did. No apology for shitting on what we had for almost ten years. No assurances that it won’t happen again, just *‘Give me another chance, Farrah.’*” The more she talked, the angrier she got.

“Are you telling me it’s not what you want?” Aaron said, reaching for her.

Farrah slapped his hand away. “You can’t just expect me to dive back into a relationship with you when you haven’t explained why you left me in the first place. ... You always did like to smooth things over; to pretend that they didn’t happen. But this did happen, and you owe me an explanation as to why,” Farrah said, hopping off the bed.

“She crossed her arms across her chest. The pose made her nipples taught against the silky fabric.

Aaron felt his dick pulsating. *Damn he wanted her! He stood.* “Alright, I’ll do my best to explain, if you’ll do something for me.”

“What?” Farrah asked as he towered over her.

He took her in his arms. “I’ve missed you,” he said, lowering his head to kiss her.

“Stop it Aaron,” Farrah demanded, twisting in his arms. “This is not the time or the place.”

“I’d say it’s the perfect time and place,” he said.

Aaron reached for a pert breast, palming the smooth globe through the silky fabric as he held her to him. “I’ve never forgotten the way you felt,” he said, grabbing a handful of her hair and snatching her head back. His mouth hungrily sought her breast.

"Stop it Aaron," Farrah said, trying to push him away from her.

"I know you've missed me too. Priscilla told me ..."

"I don't care what she told you. Get off me!" Farrah screamed, pushing as hard as she could against his chest.

Aaron picked her up effortlessly and put her on the bed, his hand over her mouth as she screamed at him. "Shhh," he said. "If you love me, we can find a way to make this work, Farrah. I know we can," he said, his lips claiming hers.

Farrah twisted under him; his weight crushing her. She felt his erection and went stock still.

"That's my girl," Aaron said, taking her stillness for acquiescence. His knee parted her thighs. He brought his mouth back down to hers.

Farrah felt weightless. She could breath again. And then, she couldn't.

Aaron stood up.

Finn.

He stood in the doorway; his blue eyes so dark they were almost black. "You got your wish," he said, as Farrah stood and squeezed the fabric of her robe to her body.

He was going to rape her. Aaron was going to rape her. Her whole body started to shake.

"Fi ... Finn," she said, her hands shaking.

"You could have at least waited to tell me that my services would no longer be needed," Finn said, disgusted that he'd talked himself into believing they had something special. That she was special.

"I didn't. We ... he-- he--" Farrah said, unable to bring herself to explain to him what had almost happened.

Finn went to the closet, retrieved his leather travel bag and began throwing things in it.

Farrah panicked.

"What are you doing?"

"My job here is obviously done," he said, angry at himself for knowing she was fresh from another man's arms, yet he still wanted her. *God he wanted her!*

"But--"

"No explanations needed Farrah Jane," Finn said. He felt like he'd stepped in a cesspool of quicksand and it was sucking him in.

Friends fucking friends like it was nothing.

Pretending to be a lover to a woman he barely knew.

A woman who sleeps with her ex-fiance with his about-to-be-new wife right down the hallway.

It was all too much. He had to get out of here.

"I hope you washed her friend off you first," Finn said to Aaron, who stood, frozen, almost like a trapped animal.

"What did you say?"

Finn ignored him. He turned to Farrah. "You should know that he's been fucking Priscilla for years. Apparently though, it's not as good as fucking you."

"Shut your mouth," Aaron said.

"Aaron?" Farrah said, turning to him.

Aaron's nostrils flared. "He's lying. Lying because he knows you want to be with me and not him," he continued, an arrogant smile hugging his face.

A white blaze of light split Farrah's vision. Had she died? People said they had an out-of-body experience when they died. They said they saw a white light. A crash brought her back to reality. Aaron was getting up off the floor, blood spewing from his nose.

"Get out before I finish the job," Finn said, red liquid dripping from his left hand.

"In case something got lost in translation – because this is apparently normal in your world – I *saw* them in the barn. To Priscilla's credit though, she swore it was the last time. Apparently she's making a life change and giving him up. But he's going to still marry Adelaide. Apparently, you'll just be fill-in sex sweetheart."

"You bastard!" Farrah said.

"Bastard? I'm the bastard," Finn said, towering over her. "Why? Because I told you the truth. You should be thanking me," he spat at her and went back to packing.

"Get out. I never want to see you again."

"The feeling is entirely mutual," Finn said as he headed to the bathroom.

"I think you broke my nose," Aaron mumbled, his hand cupping his face. Blood seeped between his fingers as he stepped into the hallway.

"My god, what happened to you?" Priscilla shrieked.

Aaron pointed, trying to explain as he sought to stem the flow of blood from his nose.

Finn continued threw a handful of toiletries into his travel bag.

Farrah stood frozen, her eyes wide, like a deer in headlights.

Farrah confronted Priscilla in the hallway just outside their suite. "Is it true?" she asked. A crowd had gathered at the commotion.

"Is what true?" Priscilla said, as Aaron wheezed in the background.

Adelaide screamed upon seeing him. "Aaron, what happened. Oh my god, what happened. You're hurt," she declared. One of her father's colleagues, a doctor, ordered Aaron to sit so he could take a look at his nose.

"Answer me," Farrah said, jerking Priscilla by the arm. "Is it true? Were you sleeping with Aaron when we were together?"

A collective gasp came from the crowd.

"You're … this is not the right time," Priscilla said. "Who told you such a tale?"

"I did," Finn said.

"You?" Priscilla said, confused.

"Yes. Me."

"But how, why…" Priscilla stammered.

"So it's true?" Farrah declared.

Finn saw the looks of pity being directed her way. In spite of his anger, he pulled her into his side. Her pain stabbed at his heart.

"She deserved to know the truth," Finn said to Priscilla.

Priscilla's anger boiled over as he he held Farrah protectively to him. "Since you're in the truth telling business, Mr. O'Hare, did you tell her all of it?"

Farrah looked up at Finn. Against her will, she slumped into him, steeling herself for another emotional blow.

"You said yourself she deserves to know the truth, so tell her Finn. Tell her who your last lover was," Priscilla continued.

At Finn's silence, she yelled, "Tell her dammit!"

"Oh god, oh god," Farrah heaved. "I'm going to be sick." She just made it to the bathroom before her stomach emptied its contents.

Chapter 24

"**D**id you know any of this?" Farrah asked.

The last hour had been a nightmare, one she prayed she would awaken from and gladly banish to the *'it was just a bad dream'* corner of her mind.

But it was all too real as Adelaide, sitting beside the on the bed beside her, attested to.

Somehow, the hallway had been cleared.

Finn was gone.

Priscilla was gone.

And so was Aaron – apparently to a private doctor to take care of his injuries. Miraculously, it was just she and Adelaide in the room she'd shared with Finn. The thought brought tears to her eyes. A couple of hours ago, she'd been in his arms. That would never happen again.

She knew she was going to miss the way he kissed her, like it was the first time every time; a once-in-a-lifetime kiss with a woman he'd dreamed about for years.

she was going to miss the way he looked at her, the blue of his eyes changing from navy to turquoise; like colors on a paint wheel you can't decide between.

But most of all, she was going to miss the way he touched her every chance he got; like being near her was a giant magnet that sucked him to her side.

Farrah felt empty, but not for the reason she would have thought just a few days ago. She felt empty without Finn.

"Yes, I knew," Adelaide said. "I found out about Aaron and Priscilla shortly after we started seeing each other."

"How?" Farrah asked.

"I investigate every man I date. In my position, you can never be too careful."

"I see," Farrah said, cupping a warm mug of lavender tea.

"I owe you an apology," Adelaide said, catching Farrah off guard. Although, after today's events, she felt like she shouldn't be surprised about anything ever again.

"It is I who owe you one," Farrah said. "I came here under false pretenses," she admitted. "My plan was to either win Aaron back, or somehow ruin your wedding. I hadn't decided which yet."

Adelaide smiled. "Under the circumstances, I understand perfectly," she said.

Farrah coughed; the tea going down the wrong windpipe at Adelaide's lack of anger. "You're way too understanding," she said, clearing her throat.

"I wish I could take that compliment in the spirit with which it was given. As I said, it is I who owe you an apology, Farrah."

"But why?" Farrah asked. Nothing was making sense any more.

"I knew Aaron was involved with you when I met him."

"You did," Farrah said.

"Yes. But it didn't matter. I fell for him almost instantly," Adelaide admitted.

"So did I."

"So that we have in common," Adelaide said, patting Farrah's hand. "I'm afraid I have this nasty habit of not caring so much about others when I make up my mind that I want something. But realistically, I knew that Aaron would never marry you."

"I think I'd come to that same conclusion, but I made peace with it. I think he gave me an engagement ring just to shut me up. Aaron is not the marrying kind; at least, he wasn't until he met you."

"Every man is the marrying kind if you dangle the right carrot in front of him. And Aaron's carrot is money."

"I don't think that's true," Farrah said. "Aaron doesn't hurt for money."

"Aaron does quite well for himself, but every trust fund baby counts on one day inheriting that trust fund. His father made it clear that unless he marries and produces heirs, there will be no inheritance."

"Why didn't he tell me that? I would have …"

"I know," Adelaide said, cutting her off. "But his father made it clear that he never would have accepted you in that role."

"But they liked me. We always got along so well. Why would you say such a thing?" Farrah asked.

The look on Adelaide's face was one she'd seen before when it was made acutely aware that she wasn't acceptable.

"It seems I really didn't know him at all," Farrah said, her eyes tearing up.

"I known we don't know each other very well, but can I be frank with you about something?"

"Don't you mean more frank?" Farrah said, blowing her nose. "I'd say we crossed the 'be frank' line at about the *I knew Aaron was involved with you when I met him'* point."

"Touche, my dear."

"Please, proceed," Farrah said, her body warmly numb as she realized there was a spike of brandy in her tea.

"While it's true that I fell for Aaron almost immediately, he pursued me too. I don't tell you this to gloat, but I don't think you're cut out for the type of man Aaron is. No woman is. But I have the thing he wants most that will keep him in line. And he was just a play thing for Priscilla. She didn't sleep with him to hurt you. It was just convenient. But she fell in love with Finn. And that tirade you just saw, it was because she realizes that he's in love with you. … And from what I saw, you're in love with him too."

"If I've learned anything this weekend, it's that love looks nothing like I thought."

"This is not your world Farrah. I spent a little time talking with your Finn, and--"

"He's not *my* Finn."

Adelaide continued as if Farrah hadn't spoken. "When I first spotted the two of you together, I couldn't take my eyes off you. For a split second, I wanted to call off my wedding."

"Why?" Farrah asked.

"Because I wanted a man to look at me the way he was looking at you. Aaron has never looked at me like that. And he never will. But I've accepted that."

"One thing this weekend has made me see is that no one should ever settle Adelaide. I think I'd rather be alone than settle."

"I don't want to take a chance that I'll never meet someone and experience what you and Finn have. Very few people are blessed to find that. It's almost like you have to win the lottery of love. And you know what your chances are of winning the lottery are, don't you?"

Farrah smiled sadly. "I see your point. But Finn … there's nothing between us. He was only a stand-in; a pretend lover for this weekend. So you see, it was all an illusion."

"What I saw between the two of you can't be faked. I've spent practically my whole life on the sidelines of love. That's why when I fell hard for Aaron, I knew I had to have him. I'm afraid I'll never feel this way again. And if I have to settle, at least there's real love on one side of the equation. But you, you have the real deal with Finn. I'd stake my impending marriage on that."

"Are you sure you want to still marry Aaron? They say there's someone for everyone."

"I know too many people who've never met their someone. I don't want to go through life alone. I have everything a young woman could want, except for a family. And I intend to have that with Aaron."

"You're very brave," Farrah said.

"More decisive than brave," Adelaide corrected. "It's too bad we didn't get to know each other under different circumstances. I think we could have been friends."

Farrah didn't know Adelaide enough to make a judgment about that. But she did appreciate her frankness.

"Can I give you some advice about Finn?"

"Why do I feel like saying no will do me no good," Farrah said.

Adelaide chuckled. "You have to take your happiness where you can find it, Farrah. Say what you will about Aaron, but I know exactly what I'm getting – and what I'm getting into. Have the courage to give Finn a chance. Aaron is lost to you; although I have a feeling that doesn't bother you one bit."

Adelaide was right. She was repulsed by Aaron after what he'd done to her. She'd go to her grave knowing that he would have raped her had Finn not entered the room. But she had the feeling that Adelaide Fulbright did indeed know exactly what she was getting into.

"I can't believe it's only been six hours since I got here. I feel like it's been six years."

"Life can change on a dime, which is why you have to go after what you want."

"The thing I want most right now is to go home," Farrah said.

Chapter 25

Eight Months Later

"I thought you'd be sipping champagne at some fancy, schmancy shindig tonight. What are you doing slumming it here lad?"

"I'd rather slum it here than sip champagne someplace else. Besides, who else is going to let me run a tab?"

"You don't need to run a tab anymore," the bartender said to Finn. "I can't pick up a paper anymore without seeing your mug in it."

"You realize you just admitted that you read the society pages, don't you?" Finn ribbed his friend.

"Hey, some of us like a bit of culture. You can't be a classless bloke all your life," his friend teased back. "And hey, if you ever lose it all, you know where to come. Your can always run a tab at *O'Reilly's.*"

"I count on it," Finn said to his favorite bartender. He took a seat at the bar – the same place he'd sat when he first met Farrah here all those months ago.

She'd never been far from his mind since that fateful day in the Hamptons, but today thoughts of her had been like rain coming through a leaky roof. Thoughts of her came in monsoons. He could even smell her, taste her and hear the sound of her voice.

The past eight months had been the worst and best of his life. He was grateful for his success. It had allowed him to live up to the promise he'd made to himself after his father died. He'd taken care of his mother. She had a nice home. He'd even bought her a car after she professed that she wanted to learn how to drive. He smiled at the hilarity of teaching her. Her joy had been his only joy these past months. He was beginning to think he'd never run into the feeling again.

"Is it still true?" a voice said from beside him.

"Is what still true?" Finn said, turning to face Farrah.

He hadn't had to turn to know who it was. Her essence had preceded her. He had known that he would see her here tonight. That's what had guided him; what had been prodded him all day long to be here tonight.

"That there are only two kinds of men – the Irish and those who wish they were?"

"You tell me Farrah Jane." Everything turned to a misty haze around her. The only thing visible through the mist was her.

"I've spent the last few months wondering about that theory."

"And your conclusion?" Finn asked.

"That you were right. That there are only two kinds men – the Irish and those who wish they were. But I'd add one caveat," Farrah said.

"The Irish and those who wish they were *with one.*"

"There are a lot of Irishmen in New York," Finn said.

"But there's only one for me."

"Do I know him?"

"You're not going to make this easy on me, are you, Finn?"

"I can't afford to." His heart hammered at his name on her lips. It had hurt too much when he'd let himself believe that he could have her. He wouldn't make that mistake again.

"I'm sorry if I hurt you Finn?"

"If?" he said.

***

She smiled as Finn ordered for them, two shots of Bushmills, single malt whiskey. "You remembered."

"Some things are hard to forget," he said. Like that first night they met. That shot of whiskey had been his entree into her world. Forgetting that would be like forgetting his own name.

"I love you Finn," Farrah said, reaching for his hand across the table.

The impromptu admission left him speechless.

It frightened Farrah, but she'd spent the last eight months scouring the core of her being for her truth. She wasn't going to shy away from it now, even if he didn't feel the same way.

"I knew I'd see you here tonight. I didn't know why, but I did," Farrah said.

"And if I hadn't been here?"

"You're pretty easy to find. I was going to come to your studio."

"Why were you so intent on seeking me out?" Finn said, refusing to let hope bloom in him again. This woman was too dangerous for his heart. He'd let hope build before. He didn't think he could afford to do it again. Was she on the rebound from her beloved Aaron? That was a fucked-up world she resided in, a world he wanted no parts of.

"Because I wanted to ask you something?"

"I'm listening," he said.

Farrah downed a hefty swallow of the whiskey.

Finn noted that she needed liquid courage. This could be good or bad. He waited. Whichever it was, it had to come from her – raw – with no prompting from him.

"Why did you tell me about Priscilla and Aaron? I've thought about it a thousand times over these last eight months. To reveal something like that; it's incongruent with who you are. You don't tell the secrets of others."

She was right. Under normal circumstances, he never would have hurt her like that. But to come back to their room; to find her in another man's arms. Lashing out physically at her wasn't an option, so he'd done the next best thing – and he'd regretted it ever since.

"I was angry," he admitted honestly. "I wanted to hurt you because you hurt me. The other part was, I wanted to shake you back to reality."

"Reality?" Farrah said.

"I knew two seconds after meeting your ex that he wasn't right for you."

"I wish I'd had your foresight. I did love Aaron, or what I thought was Aaron. Turns out, I didn't know him at all. The man I love didn't exist. So I guess in a sense, you were right."

"Emotions are a funny thing. They can make you think day is night and night is day. They can make you tell the biggest lies to yourself, and make you believe them. I knew that revenge was not what you really wanted from that weekend. It's not who you are. But it's the lie you had to tell yourself to make yourself stomach going to that wedding. The truth was too painful to admit, so you shielded yourself from it with a lie. What you were really seeking from that weekend was closure.'"

"Why didn't you just tell me that?"

"Because you wouldn't have believed me. Nobody can tell you your truth. It's something you have to discover for yourself – in your own way. On your own time."

"How is it that you knew all of this about me, but I didn't know it about me?" Farrah asked.

"My guess is that you'd never introduced the inside Farrah to the outside Farrah."

"Must you always talk in riddles? If the art thing doesn't work out, you're a shoe-in as a shrink," Farrah smiled, reaching for his hand across the table.

Finn chuckled.

"Explain what you mean by what you just said. I'm curious."

"Only that you've been so busy trying to be the Farrah that everyone thinks you should be that you've never examined for yourself what it is that you – the real Farrah – is. What she wants. What she needs."

Farrah took another swallow of her whiskey.

"Funny you should say that. It's exactly what I've been doing these last eight months – figuring out who I am and what I want."

Finn could feel Finn's walls coming down. "And?"

Farrah took a deep breath. "I wanted to reach out to you. But I knew it wasn't the right time. I had to find myself before I could even begin to think about the love I have for you – which was always there. It terrified me," she continued, the starkness of those days flooding her. "I thought, 'Wh… what if there's nothing there? What if—what if nobody loves her; the real Farr--"

Farrah's voiced cracked.

The last of Finn's walls tumbled. He moved to her side of the booth and took her in his arms.

Farrah could feel the beat of his heart. He whispered in her ear. "Tá mo chroí istigh ionat. Tá mo chroí istigh ionat," he repeated.

"I don't understand," Farrah said tearfully.

"It's Irish. Translated, it literally means, 'My heart is in you.' Or, as you Americans might say, 'I love you.' This," he said, pointing to his heart, "does not work without you Farrah. My heart lives and breathes you. Every beat. All the time."

"Oh Finn," Farrah said, raining kisses on him. "I felt a connection. I hoped. I thought it could lead … walking here tonight, I was so afraid it might be too late."

"I re-discovered something very important that fateful weekend."

"What?" Farrah asked.

"That truth always has a way of surfacing. And until you discover it and work within the confines of it, nothing will ever work."

"Like you giving into the fact that you were meant to be an artist."

"Exactly," he said, his blue eyes soft. "And that's how I knew that my love for you was real. I didn't know how or when it would manifest itself. But I've known without a shadow of a doubt since I met you is that we would always be connected."

"You really believe that?"

"The fact that we're here now is proof. All day, your essence has invaded me."

"I felt the same. I knew I'd find you here tonight. I can't explain it, but I just knew," Farrah said, feeling like she was having an out-of-body experience.

"Truth and love have their own timetable; their own way of making things connect. And it's always beautiful. Just like you, my sweet Farrah. You are so beautiful; so infinitely worth loving. And I do love you. Dear lord how I love you," he said, rubbing his thumb across her cheek. The caress was more intimate than a kiss; more cherished than a diamond.

"I wish I had recognized sooner what real love felt like. I wouldn't have wasted all that time on what I thought was love, when the real thing was staring me right in the face."

"Then let's not waste a minute more," Finn said, grabbing her coat from the booth.

EPILOGUE

“**O**h my god, I don't believe it!”

"I do," Finn said, his chin resting on the top of Farrah's head as they read the headline in the society page of The New York Times: "Billionaire Heiress Stabs Philandering Husband"

"She could have killed him," Farrah said.

"I knew when I talked to her that weekend that something was a little off about her."

"She could have just divorced him," Farrah said.

"She'll never do that. Maybe now that he's gotten the message loud and clear, he'll keep it in his pants. Otherwise, her next whack might be--"

"Finn!"

"What? I'm just saying what everybody else is probably thinking."

"God I'm so glad I left that world. Between Priscilla's messy divorce, and this with Aaron and Adelaide, I don't know how I didn't see what a messed up group of people I was surrounded by. Except for Brynwen, I don't miss a single person from that circle."

"So I take it that you don't want to settle down in wedded bliss?"

"Are you trying to ask if I want to get married, Finn?"

"I don't ever want you to be afraid to want to ask me for what you need from our love."

"I'm not; not about some things. Even though I've done a lot of work on myself, the thing I'm still most afraid of is not being really loved."

"Do you not feel my love for you? How I touch you, hold you, have to have my hands on you every time you're near? Have you not noticed that these last couple of months?"

"You're a passionate man. I-- I… just thought it was part of your nature,"

Farrah whispered shyly.

"I'm a painter, not an actor. It's not possible to fake what I feel for you. Remember the morning after the first night we met? I literally made love to you on the way out the door. I couldn't keep my hands off you until you literally weren't in front of me. I've never felt drawn to another the way I'm drawn to you Farrah. Nothing in my world makes sense without you.

Farrah eyes misted over. "Oh Finn," was all she could get out.

"So if you want to get married--"

"Farrah put a finger to his lips. "Don't," she said.

"I love you Finn. And I don't want to lose you."

"Sweetheart that would be impossible," Finn said. "You'd have to pull an Adelaide on me – only finish the job – to get rid of me."

"I can't believe you said that," Farrah said, laughing at him.

Even though his face held a smile, it didn't reach his eyes. "What is it?" Farrah said. "Be honest with me Finn."

"We had such a rocky start. I'd like to see where our love can take us on its own, without the pressure of rings and flowers and promises of forever," Finn said. He braced himself for the hurt in her eyes.

Farrah shielded her gaze from him. "All I want is you. Every day. By my side. In whatever form that takes." She looked up at him. "So I'm glad you're not ready to make promises of forever. I trust we'll get there." Farrah laughed.

It was the last thing he expected her to say. "Oh baby. I love you Farrah. I will always love you," he declared.

"And after reading the society pages, I am most certainly willing to take the long road to the altar," she laughed.

Finn squeezed her to him, joining her in laughter. "As long as we're on that road together, I'm good baby," he declared, his laugh turning to a growl as a hand slipped between her thighs.

He bent her head across his arm, his lips claiming hers.

Her shaking lips parted, sending frantic tremors along her nerves, stoking sensations in Finn he'd never known was possible from a mere kiss. And in that moment, he knew they'd reach their destination.

He was as sure of that as he was that he was an artist – and that this woman would forever be his muse.

END NOTES

If you enjoyed this novella, please recommend it to a friend and/or leave a review.

For independent publishers, word of mouth – whether it's via social media, a review, or a direct recommendation – is the best form of feedback.

It helps us to bring you more of the stories you love – at a reasonable cost.

***

Feedback

Did you feel that the characters connected in this story? Would you like a sequel? Let me know.

I can be found on Facebook at Facebook.com/InkwellEditorialPublishing and on Twitter at Twitter.com/AnInkwellPub.

My email address is inkwellny@hotmail.com.

ABOUT THE AUTHOR

I've been a reader of romance novels since I was a pre-teen. I've read hundreds of them.

"Everybody wants to be loved."

This is the enduring theme of all romance novels. We all want to be loved and accepted for exactly who and what we are.

And that's the beauty of love – it keeps the hope alive in each of us that there is someone out there, somewhere, who will love what is unique about us. This is what keeps me reading romance, after romance, after romance.

***

About Me

I've been a freelance writer – for businesses – since 1993. More about my businesses can be found below.
***

A Romance Writer Is Born

I wrote my first romance novel in 2013 (3 Weeks 'til Forever). I decided to give this type of writing a try because the title popped into my head one day and just wouldn't let go.

After finishing up several more romances, I realize that I've finally found my calling. I love reading – and now writing and publishing – love stories.

In October 2014, I formed Inkwell Editorial Publishing to bring as many stories to readers like you as possible.

I hope you enjoy reading these novels as much as I enjoy bringing them to you – whether they're written by me, or by one of our ghost writers.
***
My Businesses

New Media Words (NewMediaWords.biz) is my SEO writing company.

I also publish InkwellEditorial.com, the leading web portal for info on how to start a successful freelance writing career.

I've self-published over 50 non-fiction ebooks, mostly on the business of freelance writing, self-publishing and internet marketing.

My writing online writing courses can be found InkwellEditorial.Teachable.com.

My fiction titles (romance) can be found at InkwellEditorialPublishing.com.

Also by Yuwanda Black

A Lover for Beth
A Lover for Beth: Part I
A Lover for Beth: Part II
A Lover for Beth: Part III
A Lover for Beth: Part IV
A Lover for Beth: An Interracial Romance Box Set (Books 1-4)

An Accidental Island Wife
An Accidental Island Wife
An Accidental Island Wife: Part 2

A Taste of Tara
A Taste of Tara: Part I
A Taste of Tara: Part II
A Taste of Tara: Part III
A Taste of Tara: Part IV

Dare to Love
Dare to Love

Desperate for More
Desperate for More: Part I
Desperate for More: Part II

Hooked
Hooked! Part I

Just Sex Please
Just Sex Please: Part I
Just Sex Please: Part II
Just Sex Please: Part III

Priced Out of Love
Priced Out of Love: Part I
Priced Out of Love: Part II
Priced Out of Love: Part III
Priced Out of Love: Part IV (Cynthia's Story)

Return to Me
Return to Me: Part I
Return to Me: Part II
Return to Me: Part III

Ruthless Love
A Ruthless Love: Part I
Ruthless Love: Part II
Ruthless Love: Part III

The Affair with Mr. X
The Affair with Mr. X: Part I
The Affair with Mr. X: Part II
The Affair with Mr. X: Part III

Standalone

Harper's Heart
3 Weeks 'til Forever
Lust in Rome
Brand My Heart
Whisper of Love
SEO Examples: 10 Illustrative SEO Writing Samples
How to Make Money Writing Romance
The Brothers of Blood Gully
Love ... Up in Smoke: A Contemporary Firefighter Romance
The Courage to Love
Until You Loved Me
The Willing Captive: An Interracial, Mob Romance
The Marriage Bargain
Love after Betrayal: An Interracial, Billionaire Romance
My Stand-In Lover

Watch for more at InkwellEditorialPublishing.com.